On Suicide Bridge

Tom Dixon

Stairwell Books

Published by Stairwell Books
70 Barbara Drive
Norwalk
CT 06851 USA

161 Lowther Street
York, YO31 7LZ

www.stairwellbooks.co.uk
@stairwellbooks

ISBN: 978-1-939269-82-9

Printed and bound in the UK by Imprint Digital
Layout design: Alan Gillott
Cover art: Tom Belushi

For Sam

To Yvonne

Hope you enjoy the book!

1.

There's an Englishman, an Irishman and a priest. The joke is that they're all the same person.

Irish by birth but leaving for the bright lights of London before he was twenty years of age, he is now a man without a country. He quickly discovered there was nothing more divided than a supposedly united kingdom, where an Irish accent singled you out as either a potential terrorist or a habitual drunk.

The decades pass but the accent remains, subtly changed by his surroundings so when he returns to the place that he used to call home, his own sister struggles to understand him. She calls him a Jack of all nationalities but a master of none.

The Priest they call him. Though he may only be a priest in appearance. No one ever saw fit to ask. After all, if you've gone to the effort to dress as a priest then you must be a priest right? It was better than people assuming you were a terrorist.

He sits on the bonnet of his car looking out at the expanse of water before him. The English Channel promises France but delivers nothing more than grey waves that slap the shore below with little commitment.

Over five hundred feet down from where he stands, lay rocks that have been the last thing to embrace the fragile vessels that have thrown themselves upon them. Five hundred plus feet covered in roughly twelve seconds. His car does zero to sixty in just ten.

A member of the Beachy Head Chaplaincy Team finishes another circuit of the area and eyes The Priest warily. Though they have seen him many times, no one has yet dared approach him. The Priest watches him from behind sunglasses, the lenses tinted red.

He asked his fellow passengers to make their own way to the meeting point. Avoid public transport if possible, especially the local taxis. They seem to have a sixth sense round here.

First to arrive is Dave, his ride a silver Volvo. Dents and dings mark every panel of the car he carelessly leaves parked across two spaces. His luggage, a single battered golf club and the cans of beer he can fit in his suit pockets.

They nod a silent greeting. Dave shoulders the club and shambles towards the edge of the cliff. The Priest waves off the wary Chaplaincy

1

Team member as Dave slumps to the ground and dangles his legs over the edge. He stares out at the horizon where the North Sea joins the Atlantic Ocean.

The Priest watches Dave get up, drain a can of strong lager, place it on the cliff edge and then smash it into the sea with his club.

Another two of his passengers arrive while he watches a rambler berate Dave for littering. Aware of Dave's frame of mind, and that he does still have in his hand what could technically be described as an offensive weapon, The Priest decides not to intervene. As Dave whips out his penis and starts spraying piss onto the rocks below, the rambler wisely decides to move on.

The new arrivals both claim to be writers, of varying success but much of the same quality. Though where they're going, it doesn't really matter what your background is, they're all heading towards the same destination, roughly. You may be at the end of your rope but that's no reason not to carpool.

The more successful of the two writers saunters up to The Priest. He offers a hand towards him as his passenger wanders off to take in the view.

"Hi, I'm Matt," he says. The Priest regards his outstretched hand blankly. The finger nails are bloody and gnawed.

"Hello Matthew," The Priest replies. Matt lowers his hand and looks around the car park nervously

"I didn't realise you were Irish," Matt says sweeping his prematurely thinning hair back with one hand, a well-practiced move that has probably pulled out more hairs than it has smoothed back into place.

"Ah yes. The accent does get somewhat lost in the chat room doesn't it?"

Matt laughs, "I suppose it doesn't come up in conversation online."

"Not in a discussion group about the best way to commit suicide, no. It doesn't really seem to be the time or place. I suppose I could have littered the whole chat with some references to craic, shamrocks and leprechauns, but I feel that may have taken away from the whole gravitas of the situation."

"I thought you Irish were supposed to have a great sense of humour."

"Yeah, there are many misconceptions we Irish steadfastly refuse to adopt as a collective," The Priest leans in and whispers into his ear, "I'll let you into a secret. I don't even know what craic is. Never asked, was never told."

"Really?"

"Really. I don't think any of us know anymore. As far as anyone knows, it could have just been a bad translation from the Gaelic," The Priest shrugs.

Matt nods and wanders off to also take in the view. That's the great thing about Beachy Head; there are two things you can do here. Either take in the view or jump into it.

Matt does neither, though a man of his height and slight frame could possibly just blow right off the edge. He turns and shoots another nervous glance at the car park and up the approaching road. He stops to put his hood up and jams his hands deep into his pockets. He closes his eyes and listens to the wind whipping around him, drowning out everything but his fragmented thoughts.

There is no danger of his travelling companion blowing away. As he makes his way over to introduce himself to The Priest, his open plaid shirt flaps in the breeze, revealing a well-worn T-shirt for some old band from the nineties that strains against the beginnings of a pot belly.

"You've met Matt then," he says. "He's a famous writer, you know."

"Didn't know, didn't care and considering what we're all contemplating, can't see how it matters," The Priest shrugs.

"Fore!" Dave screams and hammers another empty can skywards. Neither rambler, nor member of the local Chaplaincy, intervenes.

The Priest hooks a thumb towards him. "That's Dave. He's not a writer."

"Like it's a badge of honour?" he laughs, "I'm just a journalist."

"Is there much difference?" The Priest asks.

"Between me and him?" he snorts. "Have you read any of his books? Christ, it's no wonder he's here."

"Not a fan then?"

"You see that Transit van over there?" He points at the rental van they'd arrived in. "The back of it's full, to the roof with copies of his last book. Not just his books in general, just that last one that sold like, a billion copies. Not that I know a single person who admits to have actually read it."

"I did say you could bring baggage," The Priest shrugs, and takes out an unopened packet of cigarettes.

"Yeah, but what kind of narcissistic arsehole brings a van-load of his unsold paperbacks with him?"

The Priest is already tearing the foil away to reveal the cigarettes inside. He plucks one from the pack and rolls the filter between his fingers.

"I dunno," The Priest replies, "I don't think it really matters."

"So what happens now?"

"We wait," The Priest says. "We still have one more member for our little cabal."

"Don't suppose I could bum a fag off you, could I?"

The Priest smiles, "It's a filthy habit."

"You can't take it with you."

The Priest holds out the packet to him. "That you can't."

So there's a Priest, a writer, a journalist and a drunk atop Beachy Head. You may have to bear with us on this.

The Priest opens the boot of his car. The drunk throws in his golf club and saunters off towards a bench where he downs another can of lager. Matt gets into the car without putting anything in the boot. The journalist also stows no cargo but doesn't get in. The Priest checks his watch.

"Do you just want to get it off your chest now?" The Priest asks the journalist.

"What do you mean?" he replies.

"I find that if a person hasn't killed themselves already they normally want to yammer on about why they're doing it before they actually do the deed. While we're here, kill some time. You want to unburden yourself?"

"Do you like your job?" he asks.

The Priest laughs. "I don't know. Do you like your job?"

Death by Monster Truck. Pursuing the Journalistic Dream. Part One

I know a lot of people say it, but I really do hate my job. I make no bones about it and will happily inform anyone who will listen about the all-consuming hatred, and outright contempt I feel, and readily display every single fucking day I have to endure working at this shitty little newspaper.

I know, it's boring and you've no doubt heard this same kind of thing said a million times before but this isn't about me hating my job. I'm like the beaten wife who runs away but always returns to the husband who kicks ten kinds of shit out of her. I mean, fuck it, does anyone really like their job?

Sadie does. Sadie loves her job. She writes for some god-awful magazine that takes people's real-life misery, types it up into a barely coherent story and presents it under a gaudy headline. I forget the magazine's title but trust me, they're everywhere. Every service station rack, supermarket shelf and council house coffee table has a copy adorning it.

Just so we're clear, Sadie is my flatmate. I have no designs on her. If it wasn't for the fact that she earns more than me and pays the lion's share of the rent every month, I probably would have moved out a long time ago. I don't 'hate' Sadie. I just find her terribly twee. Also, someone loses a lot of their desirability and mystique when you hear them being fucked roughly on the living room sofa. To this day, I can still hear her shrieks of 'Slam the clam'.

I've been single for so long now it no longer bothers me. I have added it to the ever expanding list of things that used to matter so much to me but now mean nothing.

Of late, that list has started to include living.

*

Dave has wandered into their little therapy group. He joins them with a belch but offers little else. He cracks open another tin and sits on the grass, like a child at a Punch and Judy show being performed by a troubled manic-depressive.

The journalist and The Priest fall silent.

"Nah go on," Dave slurs, "Go on and tell your story."

The journalist looks doubtful. The Priest just shrugs.

"I think I may have lost my train of thought," the journalist mumbles.

Dave grins, "I lost everything."

Dave takes one last drive. A tale of early retirement. Act 1.

I drink for health reasons or at least that was what I used to tell myself. I was a massive fan of red wine. There was nothing it couldn't do. It burns fat, lowers blood pressure, promotes long life and also is technically the blood of Christ. Come on! How can the blood of Christ be bad for you!

People say it helps in the fight against cancer as well. I don't know how it fights cancer but I can tell you, it doesn't help you in the fight against alcoholism.

I used to have a really good job. You know how you think that you have a really good job or you dream of a really good job? Well mine was better than that. I would employ you but you would be way, way down.

I'd be that guy. I'd be not your manager but maybe his manager or maybe his manager's manager. I was so high-up, if you met me it was by accident and I wouldn't know your name, let alone if you worked for me or not.

I worked hard; I played hard but also drank hard. I was going to retire whilst my contemporaries were struggling to find employment after being made redundant for being too old and too dumb to keep up. They'd be stacking shelves in a supermarket, shell-shocked whilst I knocked back another toast to my greatness.

I suppose part of that came true.

So I got my pension, early retirement and with that a lot of time to play golf. A lot of people see retirement as a great time to spend time with your loved ones. All I had at home was a wife too scared to leave me because of her irritable bowel syndrome. Plus, I really did love golf.

The drink driving tests are stupid. Everyone knows you build up a tolerance towards booze as you get older. I'm not making excuses okay, but when I was a lad you wouldn't think twice about driving home after say, four or five pints. I never killed anyone.

Not to mention, the golf course was just round the corner so it wasn't like I was driving very far. If I'd been drunk surely the barman would have taken my keys, right? Look, it's different okay. It just is. If you were in the car with me you would have been fine with me driving.

One day though, you're driving along and some cunt cuts you up, overtakes you or... or... just pisses you off, okay? The rest is like a dream... a really bad fucking dream.

*

Dave has already raised the can to his lips. He has forgotten he was speaking at all by the time the can is lowered again, too busy trying to blot out the memory he has brought forth.

"I don't think that's red wine," the journalist says.

The Priest nods in agreement.

6

"You ever had a reoccurring dream Father?"

"I'm not sure that I've had a dream full stop," he replies.

"I do. I have the same shit replayed every night it seems. Either I wake up and remember nothing or... or..."

Death by Monster Truck. Pursuing the Journalistic Dream. Part Two

I have roughly the same dream every night. I'm not sure dream is the right word though. It may actually be a nightmare. If it really happened but it keeps on replaying in your head every night is it either? I'll be damned if I know.

I suppose it is quite dream-like in a way. In the dream version, I am kind of floating outside my body watching the entire sorry episode unfold.

Selena is a friend of Sadie's. All her friends seem to have names beginning with 'S' for some reason. I don't know if this is a conscious choice or just a coincidence, I don't really care. This is my foot in the door moment. If this goes well, I can kiss my tedious post as a reporter at that shitty rag goodbye.

She leans over revealing a tantalising glimpse of her cleavage, obviously a well-practised move she uses on every sap with a cock that enters her office. "Do you know who Natalie Cassidy is?" she asks.

I snort and try to avoid looking at her tits. "The soap star?" I reply with what I hope is just the right level of arrogant cool.

"The very same," she replies, leaning back and finally giving up on involving her breasts in the conversation. It has had the desired effect though, as I now need to drag this conversation out a little longer while my erection subsides.

"Cool," I reply. It sounds childlike and insubstantial as it escapes my lips. She raises an eyebrow and regards my CV again doubtfully. "We all love Nat here. We're trying to get her to write a column for us in fact."

My mouth wants to say 'oh'. This is the level of interest this new information stirs within me. I feel my mouth forming the word as her raised eyebrow melts into a frown. She knows the one syllable answer coming. She is considering tearing Sadie a new one for wasting her time with a clueless half-wit. Some fool who can barely string together words to form a coherent sentence. Action must be taken.

"Oh... yes. She's a treasure," I say, hoping she didn't notice the pause. I nearly said 'national treasure' but she would have definitely known I was taking the piss.

It has the desired effect though, as her breasts are once again lowered to the table and she drops me a wink, "Looks like we're both on the same page then."

On a good night, I wake up around here.

*

"Is that it?" snorts Dave.

The journalist shakes his head and walks away muttering.

"You had to ruin it, didn't you Dave?" The Priest sighs, "Just as it was getting interesting."

"Wasn't that interesting," Dave replies leaning his head backwards. He stares at the cloudy sky.

The Priest shrugs. He checks his watch and taps its face with a finger. He looks up and scans the road that leads to the car park. The road is empty. He frowns.

"You got a story Father?" Dave slurs.

"Oh, I'm not here to tell stories, David. I'm merely here to listen to yours and help you all on your way. And please, don't call me Father."

Dave holds his hands up apologetically. "Sorry. What should I call you then?"

"Oh, I dunno. Anything but Father, though. I can't stand being called Father."

"So, no story then?"

"I'm afraid not, David, no. How about a joke?"

Dave grins. "A priest telling jokes. How could I say no?"

"A joke it is then David. There's a fella, religious fella trapped on the roof of his house. The streets below are steadily filling with flood water. His neighbour next door shouts up to him as he gets into his car, "Come with me," but our chap shakes his head and says God will save him. The neighbour shrugs and drives off while the guy prays from his rooftop. The water continues to rise until a man in a boat comes by. 'Come with me,' he shouts but again our friend on the roof shouts back how God will be along any moment to save him and goes back to his prayers. The man and his boat both up and out of there. The water reaches the roof some time later. Mid-prayer he is interrupted by a helicopter, dangling a rope ladder towards him. The pilot shouts, 'Come with me.' But like the other would-be rescuers he is waved away as God will be on his way any minute," The Priest takes a final drag on his cigarette, flicks it to the floor and grinds it into the grass beneath his boot, "The water rises again and the man is swept off the roof and drowns. When he reaches heaven he confronts God: 'Why didn't you save me?' God replies, 'I sent you a car, a boat and a helicopter. What else could I have done?'"

"Ha! I didn't think you were allowed to make jokes about the almighty in your line of work?"

"I don't think he'd mind, to be honest with you. It's more the eejit on the roof who's the butt of the joke anyway. If not, I'll ask for forgiveness," The Priest says with a wink.

"Forgiveness eh? Simple as that, is it?"

"Depends which church you attend, David," The Priest replies, checking the road again. "What is it you want, David? Do you want forgiveness? From me? From God?"

"Forgiveness seems to be a very simple concept everywhere but in the real world," Dave spits as he gets up and starts to pace up and down along the length of The Priest's car.

Dave takes one last drive. A tale of early retirement. Act 2.

When I retired they let me keep the company car. I lost my licence maybe a month later. I thought someone at the club must have grassed me up. The police were lying in wait. I'd just pulled out the entrance of the club, turned left and then boom, my mirrors are full of flashing blue lights.

What a moment that is. You can see why some of these idiots on the television put their foot down and make a run for it. You get such a rush.

The coward in me just pulled over though. They basically confirmed that someone had grassed on me. Didn't say who but I could've guessed. I had plenty of time to mull it over sat in the cells that night.

The car just sat on the drive. I washed it every Sunday, normally with a stinking hangover. I knew my neighbours were laughing at me. It was in the papers, only a small bit in the courts section but enough to make it the top story for discussion amongst the local gossips.

I was now reduced to having to walk to the golf course. At first I'd take the full bag but my back isn't what it used to be; last time I went I just took the one club and a pocket full of balls. Needless to say, I'm no longer the club captain.

My tastes changed as well around this time, no more merlot for me. Alcohol was virtually banned from the house so I started to hide cans of lager in the garden. These were soon discovered so I started dotting them around the housing estate where we lived as I'd often go out for long walks, plenty of time for those now I'm retired. My wife knew what I was doing but at least I wasn't propping up the bar at the local. The gossips would have had a field day with that.

I would have stopped drinking if life wasn't so fucking depressing. I couldn't function without a car. I realised I hadn't been on a bus for over a decade, the idea filled me with dread. I was trapped at home with a woman who, though I loved her very dearly, was terrified by the idea of a journey on a train because of the unsanitary condition of their toilets.

I was literally tethered to the house by her fucking irritable bowel. The stupid fucking bitch.

*

A purple Ford Fiesta pulls into the car park. It parks close to the battered Volvo but the driver doesn't get out.

"I think you should take five David," The Priest pats him on his shoulder. Dave stares blankly at the floor, his face flushed with both rage and alcohol.

The journalist returns from his walk and eyes Dave warily.

The Priest nods towards the car. The journalist returns the nod and gets in the front passenger seat.

"Maybe you should have another drink David," The Priest says.

Dave nods slowly.

The Priest crosses the car park towards the Fiesta, the driver of which has yet to emerge. The shadow inside the car remains motionless.

As he passes Dave's Volvo he runs a hand across the dented wing, the crumpled door and the scratched rear quarter panel. Where bare metal has been reached, oxidisation and the first blooms of rust have dulled the initial damage. Here and there are traces of some other cars' paint and the tar black residue of their plastic bumpers.

He approaches the new arrival and raps on the window. The shadow stirs. The window rolls down halfway.

The Priest does not stoop down to talk; he merely looks out to sea and says, "You must be Sam."

The person within remains a shadow and does not reply.

The Priest stretches and takes in a lungful of sea air. "Strong silent type eh? Well you know where we are if you're coming. We leave shortly so don't be too long."

With this he walks away. The wind carries Dave's sobs as he lies crumpled by the front bumper of The Priest's Granada, the occupants of which decide not to get involved.

He quickens his pace as Dave's cries catch the attention of one of the Beachy Head Chaplaincy Team. They arrive at the same time and eye each other with suspicion.

"Father," the volunteer says.

"My child," he replies sarcastically, "I can take it from here. Don't worry, if one of these sad sacks hurls themselves off your cliff during my watch I'll go down and get them myself."

"I'd hope we could put a stop to it before it gets to that quite frankly," he snaps back.

"I said I can take it from here," the Priest replies, "Thank you for your concern."

The volunteer eyes him suspiciously and raises his radio to his mouth.

"If you utter one word into that there radio of yours, you'll soon be picking up pieces of it from the rocks below. Honestly friend, you don't want to get involved in this."

"Are you threatening me?" he responds, puffing his chest out.

"No, friend. God is threatening you. You see my attire? I'm a fucking priest. Why am I here? I'm doing God's work. In whatever capacity, whatever situation, I am doing God's bidding. I could be crouched behind a car, answering a call of nature and curling out a big shite but still, I am doing God's work. Do I have a radio to the almighty? Do I fuck, as I already have a direct line as I'm a fucking priest. I have this, okay?"

The volunteer backs away.

"Thank you," The Priest says, turning to Dave. "You. In the car. Lap belt and dead centre."

The volunteer is already making his escape as Dave climbs into the car.

"I didn't say you could go," The Priest beckons for him to come back.

He looks terrified and makes no effort to come back quickly.

11

"I'm sorry. We both have very difficult, very stressful jobs to do and maybe I was a little off with you just then and for that I can only apologise... One moment... Just get in the fucking car David," The Priest grins and forces a laugh, "Honestly though, we're fine. Forget we were ever here. We'll be out of your hair before you know it. Besides, I'd be more worried about them over there."

The Priest nods towards a group of ramblers studying a map.

"Why?" the volunteer asks.

"Really?" he replies, taken aback. "They're clearly members of that cult, that suicide cult. You never heard of them friend? The Ram-Bula Cult. You don't want to be sat next to one of them on a plane I can tell you."

"Really?"

"All the signs are there."

"Are they?"

"That's the thing about Beachy Head nowadays; it attracts lunatics from all around the world. One of the top three suicide destinations and that's Trip Advisor saying that, not me."

"Really?"

The Priest holds up his hands, "I'm not the kind of fella to tell someone how to do their job; I get enough of that from upstairs. I'd just hate it if a simple misunderstanding meant you had to explain to your superiors why you saw fit to let ten, fifteen people jump to their deaths, whilst you were busy harassing a day trip organised by a priest for a handful of his troubled flock."

The volunteer's face first drops, then turns white.

"Can you imagine it? Firstly, Head Office aren't going to be very happy, are they? Secondly, to you anyway, is when you're faced with the almighty wrath of God after what you let happen, after I warned you about it. It'd be funny if it wasn't actually happening, wouldn't it?" The Priest smiles but it slowly melts away. "But it is, isn't it... I'm sorry, I'm rubbish with names." The Priest takes out a notebook and a pencil. He raises the pencil to his lips and wets the lead before lowering it to the paper. "What was your name again?"

"I'll be right back," the volunteer calls over his shoulder as he scuttles away.

"Take your time, my child."

A man the wrong side of middle-age emerges from the purple Fiesta. The Priest smiles, raises his hand in greeting. "Good morning," he shouts.

The man opens the boot of his car and stands motionless, staring blankly at its contents.

The Priest checks his watch and frowns.

"Will you be coming with us, Sam?" The Priest shouts. A gust of wind howls across the car park as he speaks, obliterating his words.

The Priest shakes his head and leans into the car.

"Could you two keep an eye on David please? Maybe help him with the lap belt; he has been getting awful maudlin. Would be a shame to already be a man down for our little tour," The Priest says. "I'll see if I can speed up our late arrival any."

Matt and the journalist nod in unison. Dave cracks open another can of lager.

"Where does he keep getting those?" Matt asks but The Priest is already gone, crossing the car park towards the purple Fiesta.

*

Coming with a lot of baggage has never sounded so apt. Sam stares blankly at the suitcase in the boot of the Fiesta.

Everything fell apart so quickly.

Decade old lies were being dug up.

Noise. Partially obscured noise, but noise none the less, approaches, dressed as a priest.

The past clings to him, body, soul and scent.

The long drive now reduced to a series of turns, junctions to be taken, and rotating numbers on the odometer.

The knowledge of what happened crashes head-first into his lack of knowing what happens next.

He feels old and helpless because he is old and helpless. There was always someone else there to help him make decisions, to point him in the right direction, to tell him what to do. Now they are all gone.

Slam the boot shut.

*

The Priest has gathered his flock and pulls out of the car park much to the relief of the Beachy Head Chaplaincy Team. As long as they're not leaping off *their* cliff then it's someone else's problem.

Sam remains silent.

Dave sobs.

Matt and the journalist listen.

The Priest drives. Next stop, Southampton.

2.

When does a bridge become a suicide bridge?

Simple, really, when you think about it.

For as long as people have been building structures to join one land mass to another, there has always been someone eyeing it up keenly waiting for their chance to jump off it.

Itchen Bridge, Southampton, will be the next scheduled stop and drop off point. Everyone in the car knows it will be Dave getting out, including Dave.

The journey will take over two hours. The radio is off.

They ride in silence. The minutes tick by. The Priest nervously checks his mirrors every so often, until Beachy Head is comfortably behind them.

"Are you okay Father?" Matt asks

The Priest frowns. "I'm good thank you, Matthew. How are you?"

"It's just that you keep on checking behind us. Have you seen something? Are we being followed?"

"No, Matthew, we are not. It pays to be vigilant, however, and what kind of driver would I be if I didn't check my mirrors regular like?" The Priest replies.

Matt twists in his seat to get a better look. "You'd say something if we were."

"Relax, Matthew. Maybe lay off your nails though, eh? You'll be down to the bone by journeys end."

Matt holds his hands out in front of him palms down and nods.

"Is everyone else okay back there? David? Sam?" The Priest asks.

Dave nods miserably.

Sam stares blankly out the window as Sussex whizzes by.

"How about you, Mr Journalist? We haven't heard from you in a while? You were telling us about why you hated your job so much."

Death by Monster Truck. Pursuing the Journalistic Dream. Part Three

Because of the circles I move in, virtually everyone I know works in journalism. They cover a broad spectrum of freelancers who write more for a paycheque than any particular interest in the subject they're covering. This doesn't make them bad people, just versatile. One week you are covering bass fishing, the next week some ex-footballer who has written a kids' book.

A paycheque is a paycheque after all and if you didn't write it, there would be some hungry whippersnapper just out of university who would. Possibly for less than you charge. Oh, it will be poorly written but it's not exactly art now is it? You can't be too precious about the crap you bang out on the keyboard. Otherwise, you're in the wrong job.

Sadie is a member of a group who call themselves, with no trace of irony, 'The Talent Pool.' A group of smugly self-satisfied writers whom I assumed got together to talk shop and drink expensive wine.

These frequent get-togethers are hosted randomly around fellow members' lofts and studio flats. So far, I have only had the misfortune to be in the same building as these shindigs a handful of times and up until now, have never had to actually sit in on one.

Leader of this Talent Pool is a prick called Craig. Craig writes for a magazine for men. Each month's headline is normally about some shop-girl plucked from relative obscurity that is in the possession of large breasts and low intelligence, and looks good in a bikini. That last one isn't vital as you can always Photoshop the shit out of the picture until she does.

I despise Craig more than anyone I have ever met. I doubt I will ever meet a more odious little turd and, remember, I work in journalism.

Normally I'm not invited to The Talent Pool's little gatherings but after Sadie helped get my foot in the door securing the Natalie Cassidy interview, I don't really have a choice in the matter. It can't be that bad, surely? Think of the free wine, I tell myself.

*

"And on that note," slurs Dave, pulling out a can of lager, "time for brunch."

Matt eyes him with disgust and shakes his head.

"I used to attend a few of those kind of things before I broke through." Matt says, "It's good to have people to bounce ideas off, give you a bit of feedback etcetera."

The journalist shakes his head. "Nah, it wasn't quite like that."

*

Death by Monster Truck. Pursuing the Journalistic Dream. Part Four

I enter the room and Craig's piggy little eyes regard me with suspicion.

"What's Clark Kent doing here?" he asks. Some blonde slag to his right laughs harder than necessary and squeezes his thigh.

"Oh, Craig, you are mean," the slag brays.

Sadie has made me swear that I'll behave myself. It's starting to look a lot easier said than done.

I flash a weak smile and point my finger at Craig as if it was a gun. God, I wish it were a gun. I fire off an imaginary round at him. He looks at me confused. His eyes seem even closer together today.

Sadie guides me to a chair as far away from Craig as possible, then sidles over to him, dropping into the vacant seat on the sofa to his left.

"Now then, Craig, try and behave yourself. He's not going to try to take your place as head of the pride," she says, squeezing his leg in a mirror image of what the braying slag to his right had done moments before.

"I doubt that would ever happen," he replies, arching an eyebrow in such a way it makes me want to march across the room and tear it from his face.

Sadie is looking at me as if expecting a reaction. I dodge her desperate attempts at eye contact and check out the other idiots who have nothing better to do tonight than to hang out with wanker Craig and his cronies.

Craig claps his hands together; his attempt to bring the room to order as Sadie reaches for the Pinot Noir and pours herself a large glass. I look around the room trying to ascertain who out of the assembled Talent Pool is tonight's host.

The room is bereft of personal touches altogether. Seemingly put together by a focus group or by some android interior designer. It leaves me cold, like a show home, watching clown porn alone or a mock up in a chain store furniture department.

Craig gets to his feet and surveys the room.

16

"Welcome," he says, "to The Talent Pool." He scans the room with a creepy half smile that oozes smugness. His look reminds me of a client checking out a room of whores before selecting one and defiling her on a filthy mattress upstairs.

"And welcome to my home," Craig says, opening his arms in a welcoming gesture and nodding knowingly. The fuckers applaud casually like they have just been introduced to some minor celebrity who's been paid to appear for the evening, to sign autographs, to press the flesh and maybe, for one lucky lady, a quick knee trembler behind the bins before the inevitable trip to the nearest STD clinic.

The applause helps to suppress my snigger. I should have guessed that a home as devoid of personality as this would belong to Craig. It really is his style. By style, of course I mean whatever he has been told recently is stylish. Copying it rug for rug, table for table and object d'art for object d'art. I hate him even more now.

The whole evening drags. I spot a redhead in the corner with perky tits wearing a 'Barbie is a slut' T-shirt. She has a shop-bought rock-chick vibe about her but, with tits like that, I'm not going to hold her fashion sense against her.

So far, my input has been murmured agreements, murmured shortly after everyone else has started to murmur. I'm not really listening.

I notice that the redhead barely takes her eyes off Craig but her gaze isn't reciprocated. Craig is lavishing all his attention on the blonde slag to his right, much to Sadie's annoyance I notice. Watching these stupid women fawn over a man unworthy of a hand job off a tramp is entertainment in itself. I don't need to listen.

The redhead gets steadily poutier and her eyes lose a bit of their hopeful glint as the night wears on. She starts to come close, matching me drink for drink, which is amazing really, as I am putting the free booze away like a divorcee on a hen night.

I have completely lost track of what has been said or what the whole 'meeting' thus far has been about. To be honest, I couldn't give a shit. We take five for a break just as the glowing embers of hope in the redhead's eyes finally extinguish. It's my time to shine.

I sidle over and give one final appraisal of her breasts before committing to a conversation. No one else is marking her as their territory so I move in.

"I hear Sindy's worse," I comment, pointing a finger at her boobs.

She laughs in a well-practised guffaw. A laugh she must use often when men pass comment on the statements printed upon the taut fabric that adorns her chest.

I can tell her eyes are searching for Craig as she over-embellishes her laugh so more than a few people in the room turn their heads to the apparent mirth making I have caused.

"It would be a complete different story if Ken paid her a little more attention though eh?" I was going to go with an ill thought out joke questioning Ken's sexuality, but I think it unfair to question the sexuality of a man with no actual genitalia for a cheap joke.

Her eyes slide away from Craig and finally focus on me. Yup, I'm in here.

Before my new friend and I can get too cosy, Craig reconvenes our little get together. Placed on all our seats is a stack of awful magazines much like the one Sadie writes for.

Top of the pile boasts the headline, 'One-armed paedo raped me in his sex den' with the equally awful sub-headline of, 'Evil Ryan lured me with lies.' I snort dismissively, much to Craig's annoyance.

"Something funny," he asks.

I wave the magazine in the air, "It's just the headline. Does it make it any worse he only had one arm? And this 'he lured with lies' part. It's pretty unlikely he would have lured her with his faultless logic, isn't it?"

The room falls silent, leaving me smirking to myself. The seconds stretch out uncomfortably.

"I'm sorry, am I missing something here?" I ask, losing the stupid smirk.

"Sadie?" Craig says, turning to my flatmate dramatically. He now sports an equally cocky smirk, very like the one I was rocking. "Could you be so kind as to fill your friend in."

Sadie is doing very well at masking her anger and fixes me with a smile that promises harsh words later, maybe even a full-blown argument.

"Have you seen how many of these magazines grace our newsstands, newsagents, etcetera? Most of the ones you will see tonight are published weekly and packed with true crime, crosswords, adverts for crisps and um... real-life stories."

The group release a collective titter to which Sadie smiles and nods knowingly.

"As farfetched as an episode of Eastenders and as equally made up, I'm afraid. You see, we Talent Poolers are the largest writers' collective producing these 'real-life stories' in London. If you're reading about a limbless teenager raped by the spirit of her deceased Rottweiler, it is more than likely that we penned it."

"You must be very proud," I sneer.

"Not really, but surprisingly well paid."

Craig butts in. "And this is where you come in."

"I'm good, thanks," I reply tipsily.

"Ah, but you're not, though. Sadie has been telling us... moaning to us on and off for... for what seems like forever. Doesn't it seem like forever?" he asks the room who nod and murmur in agreement, bar Sadie who is studying her sandals with fierce concentration.

I fix Sadie's bowed head with a steely glare. "What exactly has dear Sadie been saying?"

"Just how finances can be, ahem, tight some months when it comes to bills etcetera. There is no shame... well, not that much shame in it. We have all found ourselves at some point raiding the penny jar." Craig's smirk is replaced by what I am sure he considers his 'serious' face, "But is it fair when you start dipping into Sadie's penny jar?"

"Is this about money?" I say, trying to get Sadie's attention. She couldn't look more sheepish if she donned a fleece and was fighting off the attentions of an amorous farmer, "Sadie? If it's money you should have said something."

"It's every month," Sadie says, looking up at last. Eye contact is minimal.

"You said it was alright?" I snap back.

"Yeah, well it's not," Craig butts in yet again as he slips a comforting arm around Sadie.

"I don't remember asking you, you fucking lizard." I regret this slip instantly as Craig feigns looking hurt while the rest of the room gasp in shock.

"I just want to help a friend. You're taking advantage of Sadie's good nature," Craig, king of mock concern replies. I'm sure the bastard knows all about taking advantage of vulnerable young women. I decide that it may not be wise to vocalize this particular thought though.

"Craig just wants to help," Sadie butts in before I can say anything else.

"And we can help you as well," Craig adds, attempting a friendly smile that just turns into the annoying smirk he usually sports.

I nearly say, 'I'm fine' but obviously in their eyes I am far from fine. I am left speechless. I'm not sure if I'm shocked or just too furious to speak. I have no choice but to keep schtum and listen to their plan. The redhead in the 'Barbie is a slut' T-shirt scrapes her chair closer to me and places a reassuring hand on my knee.

"Let us help," she smiles weakly, regarding me as if I'm a decrepit pensioner refusing to move into a nursing home. I close my hand over her tiny, pale hand and offer her what I hope is a warm smile and a

19

nod. Her tits still look spectacular. I start thinking about what her nipples may look like.

*

"So you had to write a few fluff articles," Matt shrugs. "I had to do a lot worse to get where I am today. You don't see me crying about it."

The Priest laughs. "What are you crying about then, Matthew? We're all here for the same reason remember? You do understand that though your death may temporally improve your sales, you'll be somewhat incapacitated... somewhat dead to enjoy it. What brings a famous writer like yourself to this side of the abyss?"

"I see no other choice."

"Care to elaborate?" The Priest asks.

The man from the returns department. A short story in two parts. Part One.

My wife always resented me. It wasn't my fault I won. I'm one of life's winners. I couldn't do a nine-to-five job anymore, I would literally go insane. I am a writer.

Sadly though, so was my wife.

When we met we were both aspiring writers. She was writing some dreadful chick-lit book, while I was dabbling in young adult fantasy. It was going great. But then she got pregnant.

I love my children. No one can say otherwise but at that point in time it was definitely not part of the plan.

Some hard decisions had to be made. Children are not cheap after all. I suppose it all came down to the money. We are both very driven people, so neither of us wanted to give up on their dream of making the big time.

We came up with a deal. We would both finish our latest works and submit it to publishers. Whoever sold the most books would pursue their dream; the other would stay at home and raise the kids.

Like I said, though, I am one of life's winners. She didn't stand a chance.

I don't need to bore you with the rest of my rise to fame. There was a point when you couldn't pick up any magazine without there being some article or interview with me somewhere within its pages.

That book was my making and my undoing, with a little help from the man from the returns department.

At first I thought it was a joke. A trick dreamed up and orchestrated by one of my old university chums, maybe.

It wasn't.

I was in my study at home writing when there was a knock at the door. I don't answer the door unless I'm expecting someone, so I ignore it. I'm three flights up so I'm not stopping mid-sentence on the latest masterpiece to tell a gypsy I don't want to buy any of her pegs.

The knock comes again. I shout for my wife but I know she popped out for a play-date with the kids and won't be back until much later.

I hear the creak of the letterbox and then something hitting the floor. I think nothing more of it. Probably something needed signing for. I can collect it later when I'm not busy writing.

I stop for a cup of tea about half an hour later.

As I head downstairs, I see what's been posted through the letterbox. Not mail, but three dog-eared copies of my last book.

I stoop down and pick them up, casually leafing through them before dropping them in the recycling tub in the kitchen. Obviously someone thinks they're some kind of comedian.

I think nothing of it until the next day when again, someone knocks at the door.

I pause, but I'm writing. No distractions.

The letterbox creaks again and something hits the floor, though this time it sounds like a lot more.

Oh, I try going back to my writing but after what happened the previous day, I can't.

I spend five minutes writing and then deleting the same sentence until I just have to go and check.

Lo and behold, someone has posted more books through my letterbox, six of them this time. I scoop them up and open the front door, checking the street which is now virtually empty except for an old woman walking her dog.

I go back in and again I dump the books in the recycling. I don't write anything for the rest of the day. My wife asks me what's wrong but I don't tell her what's bothering me. After all it's just someone's idea of a joke, right?

Wrong. Day three and I'm waiting by the door. He hasn't even finished knocking before I fling the door open and confront him.

"Okay, who put you up to this? Was it Toby?" I demand.

The man produces a card from his shirt pocket and holds it out to me; not offering it, merely showing me his credentials.

"I am from the returns department. I believe these are yours." He pockets the card and picks up a carrier bag off the floor. The bag is packed carefully and to the top with copies of my last book. He holds it out to me.

"The joke's over now, you can go tell Toby that I've rumbled him."

The man from the returns department frowns. "I don't know any Toby, I'm afraid. I am quite busy today so if you could just take your books then I can be on my way."

He shakes the bag at me.

"I said that's enough," I snap back.

"Sir, are you the author of these books?"

"Yes."

"Then these are your books."

I sigh and snatch the bag from him. "Whatever, you can tell Toby though, that if he does this again tomorrow there isn't a chance in hell I'm ever going to read his screenplay."

I then slam the door shut on him.

Later that evening my wife asks me why I have a carrier bag full of my novels in the kitchen. I mumble something about a project in reply. She asks me if I'm feeling okay.

I get a couple more hours in at the keyboard before going to bed. My wife asks me why the recycling bin is full of my books. I pretend to be asleep.

The next day I take the carrier bag to a local charity shop but return home to a welcome mat covered in yet more books. As I hurriedly pick them up, my wife returns from yoga. She doesn't say a word.

That afternoon I leave Toby an angry message on his voice mail and then go to meet my agent.

The meeting does not go well. To be honest, my mind is elsewhere, whilst my agent is only concerned about when the next book will be ready.

I return home and find my wife in the kitchen. A bottle of wine sits atop the counter, half a glass left inside.

She explains how she is worried about me. She is concerned about my behaviour of late. Is there anything I want to tell her?

I tell her about deadlines. I may have shouted it actually. I tell her about the pressure of fame and the demands that are made of me on a daily basis.

She asks me if I'm drinking again or, worse, on drugs.

I tell her I'm going to bed.

As I turn to leave she says that Toby rang.

I stop.

Toby was confused. I'd left a rambling, threatening voice mail, he'd said.

I tell her that I will ring him in the morning.

As I slam the kitchen door I hear her say that she loves me.

She never says it again.

*

"They pulp them, you know. Charity shops rag them but it's all the same. They all get pulped. All those reality T.V ghost-written shit memoirs all end up in the same place," the journalist butts in.

Matt remains silent. Tears roll down his face.

"Then they become the new best-seller, and I say that in the loosest of terms, by the latest reality star or some tie-in panel show hardback. Everyone knows that."

Matt wipes his eyes with the sleeve of his stripy hooded top and scoffs. "What do you know? Everything you write gets binned."

"Oh, let's not start on whose writing is the more disposable."

Matt lunges towards the journalist but is blocked by Sam.

Sam pushes him back into his seat and says, "Are you trying to get us killed?"

The Priest laughs. "Thank you, Sam. Please remember the car is a no fighting zone."

"He started it," Matt mutters.

"You never finished your tale, did you?" The Priest says. "You left us pondering what a redhead's nipples look like. I think Matthew may need a minute."

"Ah, the redhead," the journalist laughs.

Death by Monster Truck. Pursuing the Journalistic Dream. Part Five.

The evening wears on. I get increasingly drunk. The redhead gets increasingly friendly and the entire, awful plan unfolds before me.

I agree in principle – not that these fuckers seem to understand what principles are – that, when needed, I will help them out writing their awful little stories. Like a very low rent script doctor of sorts.

In all honesty, it doesn't really matter because as soon as I nail this Natalie Cassidy interview, I will be inundated with further interviews and be able to toss more than my fair share of the rent into Sadie's stupid fucking face. Fuck it. I may be able to move out altogether. That'll teach the scheming little bitch.

Thankfully, the whole 'intervention' feel of the evening has been replaced by a much happier one involving dreadful ideas for articles being tossed back and forth, excessive drinking and a little bit of cocaine making the rounds.

There is even time for a jovial brainstorming session regarding probing questions for Miss Cassidy's interview tomorrow, which I hurriedly jot down into my battered reporter's notebook as the redhead's hands begin to explore further afield than my knee.

I try a line of coke. Not something I often dabble with, but when I'm drunk I'm up for anything, be it drugs, new positions or voting Lib Dem.

The evening speeds up. The redhead and I stumble down the steps of Craig's apartment and into the crisp night air, giggling like a pair of idiots ripped to their tits on booze and coke that has been cut with Vim.

She starts pawing at the front of my trousers like a dog pawing at a door in the rain as soon as we get into the back of the taxi. The driver is all leers as I mumble my address to him and cup one of her firm breasts with the arm I have slung around her shoulder.

Initially I am a little wary of the taxi driver's stare, more out of personal safety than his obviously keen interest in voyeurism. But, as he manages not to crash into anything and keeps the vehicle in a roughly straight line – after all, this is a taxi driver and not a driving instructor, so certain rules like using your indicators don't apply – I'm more than happy to let him watch as long as he doesn't whip his cock out and try joining in.

Things start to hot up as she fumbles my fly open and manipulates my manhood in a way reminiscent of a plumber trying to fix an overflowing plughole with a plunger. Her technique leaves a lot be desired, but thankfully she enlists the use of her mouth instead and the whole experience becomes pleasurable again, albeit briefly.

I've not emptied my nuts for quite a while so I empty my load faster than a fly-tipper in a lay-by, much to her surprise, but not as surprising as what happens next.

I look down at her to see her clearly struggling with the decision to either spit or swallow.

"Don't you dare, sweetheart," the taxi driver barks, fixing me with an angry look in his rear-view mirror. All the sexy, dangerous voyeurism has drained from the moment. I am now just a pissed bloke with a rapidly softening semi, exposing himself to a middle-aged taxi driver.

Bless her, she tries to swallow my mess but she just can't do it. She looks up at me from my lap and starts to choke and gag, reminding me of my parents' St Bernard dog after it had pounced on a red-hot sausage that had just fallen from the grill. The greedy beast had tried to gobble it down in one huge bite, before its sensitive oesophagus rejected it in a projectile fountain of Pedigree Chum and stomach acid all over the kitchen floor.

Childhood memories are made of these cherished moments.

It all happens very fast but when my dreaming brain replays it, it all happens very slowly, played out in painful slow motion until the taxi driver angrily pulls away from the curb.

She knows it. I know it. The fucking taxi driver knows it. It's all a question of when and where it's going to happen.

She convulses one final involuntary spasm, and then unleashes her dinner, numerous glasses of wine, and other recently ingested and partially digested delights directly over my still exposed genitals.

The taxi driver jerks the steering wheel hard left and the car mounts the pavement, before screeching to a halt.

"Out. Now," the taxi driver barks as he gets out of the vehicle and aggressively pulls the door nearest to us open.

The redhead is now in tears. I am torn between comforting her and screaming at her for puking in my lap. I have little time to do either, as the driver grabs me by the scruff of my T-shirt and drags me from the car and onto the pavement.

"I'm sorry, I'm sorry," she mumbles, getting out the other side. A few small chunks of vomit cling to her chin,

The taxi driver is back in his cab and tearing away back up the road before we know it.

On the upside, he didn't charge us for the ride. On the downside, I am stood in a densely populated residential area with my trousers around my ankles. My flaccid penis slowly dripps the remnants of vomit onto the pavement below, while the redhead sobs, sitting where the pavement meets the gutter.

"Are you okay?" I ask, knowing the answer.

"No. I am not fucking okay," she snaps back. Her make-up is destroyed, her T-shirt speckled with orange hued vomit.

I stand dumbfounded. What can I say? I pull up my trousers. There is vomit in the hair around my balls.

Our little performance hasn't merited a single twitch of the curtains from any of the surrounding houses. It joins the long list of things people don't do anymore, like answering the phone, answering the door, or wondering why next door's burglar alarm is going off.

The redhead pulls out her mobile phone and starts stabbing at the buttons.

"Who're you calling?" I ask nonchalantly.

"Craig," she replies, lifting the phone to her ear.

"Craig? Why are you calling Craig?"

"He's my boyfriend," she says, regarding me as if I am the stupidest man alive.

"Oh," is all I can manage in reply.

I am the stupidest man alive.

The occupants of the car nod in unison, even Sam.

Matt shakes his head. "Didn't see that coming."

"Nor did I, Matt, nor did I," the journalist replies.

Silence descends. The bumps on the road become the car's soundtrack. The radio is still off.

The Priest catches Dave's eye in the rear view mirror.

"Your stop is coming up soon, David. Do you want to finish off your tale? I sense there is a bit more to your predicament than a dependence on the old sauce and a lack of transport."

Dave rubs his stubbly jaw with his hand and searches for a beer that isn't there.

"I don't suppose any of you have anything to drink, do you?" he begs, but no one does.

"You'll be fine without the Dutch courage, David," The Priest replies.

Dave takes one last drive. A tale of early retirement.
Act 3.

My wife told me it was for my own good. She'd only done it because she loved me, because she was worried, the kids were worried – oh, everyone was so fucking worried.

Early retirement on paper sounds great. You work even harder now to finish earlier. It's a joke. Unless you're in your mid-twenties, early thirties, retirement is a complete waste of time and time is something you now have a lot of.

One of the local kids had found one of my stashes and had proceeded to drink it. It was only four cans of lager but the kid was seven years old. The parents panicked and rushed him to the local hospital where they pumped his stomach as a precaution. At his age I would have taken a sip and spat it out. I bet he'd got a taste from it from his dad, he looked the type. There's no way a kid would just drink four cans of lager is there?

The kid did and though no one directly said it, I knew tongues were wagging and fingers were pointing. Of course, they were mainly pointing at me.

Those cans could have been anyone's.

The kid's fine. Doubt he'll be touching another drop for a long time. You could say I'd done him and his parents a favour. The wife didn't see it like that.

The whole sorry affair had obviously taken its toll on me as well, not that anyone cared about that. In fact, I'd barely touched the stuff that day.

She was in a mood. Dinner had been eaten in silence and that was continuing into her doing the washing up.

I sat in my chair and watched the local news as she bashed pots and pans around in the sink. I thought about going out and stretching my legs.

Next thing I know, she's behind me, dishcloth in one hand asking me if we are just going to ignore the elephant in the room. I laugh and tell her not to call me an elephant. I see tears in her eyes.

She asks me questions without waiting for answers. Why this and why that. Then she finally gets to the obvious root of the problem. The embarrassment it causes her.

I grab my chance and berate her. I effectively imply my drinking is her fault.

She says she wished that she had never called the police in the first place.

I don't understand.

That at least if I'd wrapped myself round a tree and died she wouldn't have to be the butt of people's jokes around the estate. She tells me that people are calling me 'Thirsty Dave.'

I ask who.

"Everyone," she replies.

I ask what she means about her calling the police.

She tells me to shut up.

I don't shut up though. What does she mean? Though I already know exactly what she's done. I just want to hear it from her stupid mouth.

She is now sobbing but I ask again, what does she mean? I scream it so loud that I already know them next door are calling the police.

She screams back that it was her. She was the one who tipped the police off. That she only wanted to help. That everyone was so worried. That she didn't know what else to do. That she did it for my own good.

I call her a stupid bitch, take my car keys off the hook by the front door and leave the house.

I drove for hours. I was just so angry with everyone.

3.

The Priest focuses on the road ahead. The rest of the passengers remain silent. Dave silently dares them to comment.

His threat is the silent threat of a drunk, though, squaring up to either a minor or invisible foe.

He wipes the spit from the corner of his mouth roughly with the sleeve of his suit jacket. The spittle, white and concentrated, like foam, joins the streaks of mucus and remnants of condiments that already stain his cuffs.

The silence demands he finishes his story.

Dave takes one last drive. A tale of early retirement. Final Act.

What happens next is more a failing of society than a reflection on me, okay?

I push the accelerator to the floor. The roads blur past. I don't feel any better but, fuck it, fuck it all, eh?

I barely make a corner and feel more alive than I have in – what? – maybe twenty years? I feel the wheels skip out from under me, searching for purchase, traction, whatever. I'm pushing this car to its fucking limits.

I'm still in control though. I have this machine, this monster, at my command and I'm still its fucking master. I'm in charge. I'm still the boss.

And why not? Regardless of my job title, or lack of nowadays, I'm still pushed to my limits every fucking day. Go me!

As I said, I drove for hours. At some point I had to refuel and maybe I'd bought a half bottle of vodka while I was there. If anything, I was going to drink it before I went to bed but fuck knows when that was going to be.

I may have drunk it before... I may have drunk it after... I can't remember... and that is the truth.

Down one of these featureless lanes I swing my Volvo and behind me this Audi suddenly appears. It flashes its high beams at me and gets real close to my bumper.

I slow down; a real dick move, yeah? But still this fucker is nearly kissing my bumper.

They try overtaking me but I pull out. BAM! I make contact and it feels fucking good, like punching your wife in the face. Know your fucking place, bitch.

Hitting them seems to make them more skittish but I'm having fun now.

They accelerate hard to get past me but I'm soon right behind them and start to nudge their bumper. I'm not going to lie, it felt <u>really</u> good.

I ran them off the road. It wasn't something I planned but that was how it happened.

I left them in a ditch, steam billowing from the engine bay and waited for the police to come knocking and take me away.

The following day I wake up in a supermarket car park, still a free man. My head hurts no worse than any other hangover of late but my back protests about being made to sleep in a car.

I get out and walk around the car, taking in the damage. One thing's for sure; it wasn't a dream.

The thing that really leaps out at me, though, is the driver side door. Not the dents, scratches or dirt though. What I notice is the clustered paint chips around the door handle. I squat down and look at them closer. The surrounding area looks like a teenager's pock marked face.

I stare at those little nicks for a long time, dumbfounded at what may have caused them, forgetting about everything else until a van driver walks past me devouring a bacon sandwich.

When I pull the car into the driveway back home some hours later, I can already feel the gaze of the local busybodies watching me. The house is empty. No note has been left. No one has been back.

I lock the front door, hang up my keys and sit in my chair. At some point I fall asleep. I don't dream, though. It's one of those daytime lapsing in and out, drenched in sweat, just waiting for the police to kick down the front door kind of naps.

Just after it starts getting dark I'm awoken by a car driving by, the headlights illuminating the room briefly in a flash of brilliant white. I am still alone in the house.

I get up and walk from room to room, taking it all in sober and in the dying light. Bar the money in the joint account and the ruined car in the driveway, this is what I have to show for my time on this earth so far.

There is nothing for me here anymore.

I take the keys off the hook and leave.

The night takes me back down the same roads and I soon find myself back at the crash site. To my horror, I can tell the car is still there, undiscovered amongst the undergrowth.

I flee again, stopping at a petrol station and refuelling both the car and myself. The shock has really taken its toll so I also get a small bottle of brandy.

I find myself parked on an industrial estate on the outskirts of town. I drink the brandy – it's only a small bottle – and stumble to a nearby payphone.

The anonymous phone call to the police doesn't go well. I have no idea where the car crash happened, even if the road has a name, and I'll be damned if I just lead them there to be taken away in bracelets.

Eventually I give up. Fire up the Volvo and wake up the next morning in the same place I had the previous.

I return to the crash site again. This time it is a lot lighter and not only can I make out the car is still there but that there are still people inside as well. I get back in the car and flee.

When I feel I have put a safe distance between me and the crash, I pull over and frantically search an old road atlas for the name of the road.

Another garbled exchange between me and the police operator ensues. I keep it brief as I can; I'm terrified that they're tracing the call.

Convinced I will be arrested at any moment, I drive to the shops and fill the boot with enough alcohol to kill an elephant. I head back home, determined that regardless of what my wife says I'm sleeping in my bed one last night.

It doesn't matter anyway; she hasn't even come back for clothes. The house is still as deserted as when I left it the last time.

The next day is lost to me. I pieced it together using our computer's search history. Obviously I'd started drinking pretty early; who wouldn't in my situation? The rest of the day it looks like I looked up the meaning of various legal terms: vehicular manslaughter, death by dangerous driving and the definition of murder were the ones that leapt out. Later I searched maps of the area the crash had happened. After midnight I'd searched about the best way to commit suicide.

I visited the crash site one last time.

Of course, the car was still there.

This time I got out. I followed the path of destruction the Audi had ploughed through the undergrowth until it slammed into its final resting place.

The front of the car had taken the brunt of the impact. The tree it had hit was entwined with the metal and plastic of the car's destroyed grille and engine bay. Fluid dripped from various places, black oil, blue anti-freeze and red blood.

The driver was dead. The airbags had deployed and now lay limp from the pillars and steering wheel. The speed they had impacted at made them of little use.

The passenger, though: she was still alive. As I peered through the cracked glass of the windscreen her eyes fluttered open. She sees me and raises a blood encrusted arm towards me. She manages to stretch out a quivering finger and point towards me, opening her mouth to speak but nothing but a moan escapes.

I ran.

That was two days ago.

Now I'm here.

*

Itchen Bridge beckons.

There are no official records regarding the number of suicides from this bridge. It isn't something they want to advertise, nor does any bridge. Rarely are bridges built with any thoughts toward the prevention of suicide. Such measures are an expense no one wants to acknowledge or pay for. Build the bridge, take the money, and let the local council worry about the long-term implications. You never know, maybe they'll call you back with the contract for the alterations. Repeat business never hurt anyone.

From the designer's point of view, no one wants to add high sides, cumbersome anti-this and that deterrents to their sleek, modern design. Unless you have worked in a sly diving board somewhere or included an 'End it all here' sign in the design mock-up, you're probably going to be fine. After all, you're a designer not a health and safety officer.

Freedom of information doesn't encompass such facts like who was the first known jumper. Nor does it tell you how many people per year jump. No one is obliged to tell you. The police have no crime to record, hospitals don't count the incoming dead and without a body who can say you're dead in the first place?

It's not like you're advertising your intentions. The last thing a truly suicidal person wants is to be stopped.

For ease of access, Itchen Bridge is a great candidate.

Before the bridge was built, the best way across the River Itchen was the nearby Woolston Floating Bridge. Technically, this was a ferry but, after over a hundred and forty years of calling it a bridge, no one was going to be that petty. As the new bridge opened in 1977, the old 'bridge' quickly shut up shop and the ferries were decommissioned.

There had been three ferries running. One of them was later turned into a nightclub that one night burnt to the ground.

They had named the club 'Floaters.'

*

"So here we are, David," The Priest says, rubbing his hands together for warmth, "mere feet away from a new beginning."

The engine of the old Ford Granada clicks in the background, cooling down from the first leg of its marathon jaunt.

Dave looks scared, confused, and every inch the alcoholic he is.

"I'm sorry," Dave mumbles.

The Priest nods. "That's a start, I suppose."

"Help me."

The Priest smiles and says, "I'm showing you the choices, David. You can't go home again. Part of me reckons you can't give up the booze either. Part of me reckons that by moving you eighty miles away from your car, we have removed the deadliest weapon from your hands. I have been known to be wrong on occasion, however."

"So what do I do now?" Dave asks.

The Priest shrugs. "As long as you don't implicate me in any of it, you can do whatever you please."

"But I killed people."

"Indeed you may have. Can you live with that? Don't answer, I don't care. I'm merely, ha, I'm merely a man dressed as a priest."

"Will God forgive me?" Dave asks.

"He might. I'd be more bothered about their parents, siblings, and friends, though. After all, they're normally the ones who seek violent and bloody retribution."

"That seems pretty unfair."

"Life is unfair," The Priest says. "Kill yourself or get over it."

*

The Priest gets back into the car.

Dave weaves his way towards Itchen Bridge.

"Do you think he'll go through with it?" Matt asks.

33

The Priest winces. "No, Matthew, I don't. I think he'll be one of these sad sack men shuffling around the country you see from time to time, sleeping rough and drinking themselves to death."

"Then why bring him here?" Sam asks. He stretches his legs, clearly enjoying the extra space.

"Why not? Everyone needs a start point. Why shouldn't David start his next chapter here or, if he feels like it, end it here? Isn't that what bridges are for? You bridge a gap between two different places. But wouldn't it be nice if he had a third option. One in the middle, so that if he so felt inclined, he could just jump off and just get the fuck out, on his terms for once."

Matt wags a finger. "Ah, I get your angle. You're the mysterious priest who picks up the suicidal and shows them how life is so much better with them in the world. I've got your number."

The Priest smirks. "I doubt that very much, Matthew. Maybe you should spend a wee bit more time about thinking about what's brought you here than trying to fathom me out."

He fires up the engine and pulls away.

They pass Dave on the bridge.

No one looks back.

*

It gets easier when Southampton is behind them.

The problem with a story told to you by a drunk is you can never be sure what is true. Oh, there will be truth in the tale, but it'll be more embellished than the collection of medals on a dictator's chest.

"Next stop, a slice of history. The Clifton suspension bridge, Bristol," The Priest says breaking the silence.

Sam stares out the window.

The journalist stares at his hands while Matt gnaws at his.

"So which of us is getting out there, priest?" asks Sam.

The Priest shrugs. "Doesn't matter, really. Maybe I'll get out."

Sam narrows his eyes. "I don't get you."

The Priest smiles. "I'm quite the enigma, right? Be great for the next best-seller, eh, Matthew? You could write a character about a mysterious priest or some shite."

"Fuck off," Matt spits back.

"Oh come on now, Matthew, there's no need for profanity. Don't you like best-sellers?"

"Just fuck off, okay. I won't talk to you about being a priest if you don't talk to me about being a writer," Matt replies.

The Priest considers this. "I'd be quite interested to hear your views on the priesthood if I'm honest with you."

"Or we could just listen to the radio," Sam chips in.

"Way to change the subject Sam," The Priest laughs. "Radio's broken anyway."

The journalist squints at the stereo. "Does the tape deck work?"

"Yes. Yes it does," The Priest says.

"Do you have any tapes?"

"No. No I do not."

"Ah," he sighs.

"So that will be all avenues of entertainment exhausted bar the telling of tales," The Priest eyes the journalist in the passenger seat. "Your tale was just getting interesting."

"Was it? Where was I again?" the journalist asks.

"As I recall, you're stood in the street, pants around your ankles, privates covered in puke."

The journalist nods. "Like I could forget."

"Do we pick up the story there, then?"

The journalist shakes his head. "Oh no, I don't even remember how I got home after that. The police never got involved, so at least I can guess I pulled up my pants at some point."

"So what do you remember?" asks The Priest.

"The next day is pretty etched in my memory..."

Death by Monster Truck. Pursuing the Journalistic Dream. Part six.

"You reek of alcohol," Sadie says as she wafts through the kitchen.

I'm sat at the table with a taste in my mouth I struggle to describe, but that is no doubt akin to that of an area that woodland creatures have designated as their toilet.

"Fuck off," I mumble as the world continues to throb and pulsate around my pulverised brain.

"Good night?" she asks with a sly smile.

I ignore her and ask, "Why didn't you mention to me that the redhead I was getting friendly with is going out with that prick mate of yours?"

"Everyone knows they have an open relationship," she says breezily. I want to beat the breeziness from her.

"Everyone in your little group knows you mean. I didn't have a clue."

"Oh, what does it matter?" She ruffles my hair jovially.

I nearly tell her to fuck off again but decide to conserve my energy instead. After all, today is the Natalie Cassidy gig.

"I'm surprised you caned it with such... vigour last night," Sadie says as she sits at the other end of the table. I don't blame her for keeping her distance, as I'm sure anyone could get inebriated inhaling the fumes working their way out of my pores this morning.

"I can handle it," I lie. I cannot handle it. Vomiting is inevitable and not just a possibility this morning. I really hope that Sadie will have fucked off by then. Spare me the embarrassment of her listening to me shouting chunks into the toilet later on.

"Why are you in such a good mood this morning anyway?" I ask, just as the toilet down the corridor flushes, as if it meant to answer my question before she could answer it herself.

The bathroom door opens and out steps Craig, clad in Sadie's salmon coloured bathrobe, my toothbrush sticking out one side of his mouth.

"Any chance of a coffee?" he asks smugly before ducking back into the bathroom.

I'm speechless. The likelihood of impending sickness increases tenfold as Sadie gets up and slops the dregs from the cafetiere into the sink. The sound of the brown, stewed sludge hitting the sink makes my stomach perform cartwheels.

I know she is waiting for me to say something so I let the room descend into silence. What am I expected to say? Well done Sadie! You have embarked on a one-night stand with an odious turd. Bravo that girl, someone give her a big hand. Hopefully a big open hand, delivered swiftly across her stupid fucking face.

She finishes her preparations and brings over the fresh coffee. I can feel her guilty little eyes probing me for the slightest hint of a disgusted outburst.

Finally, she cracks.

"Well, say something then," she demands. Her fringe shakes as she speaks. It only ever shakes when she is angry.

"It's your vagina. Put whoever you want in it," I reply curtly, reaching for a coffee. She slaps the hand away.

"That is for Craig."

"Lucky bloody Craig."

"Look, what is your fucking problem?"

"He is the fucking problem Sadie," I hiss, trying to keep my voice as low as possible; wouldn't want to upset the guest after all. "Of all the fucking people. You may as well have brought…"

"Oh, save the witty simile for someone who gives a shit," she butts in venomously.

I am stunned into silence. I had always thought my witty similes were one of my few redeeming features.

"I don't have time for this bullshit," I mutter as I push away from the table. The resulting noise from the chairs legs scraping across the kitchen tiles nearly shakes the fillings from my fragile skull.

I march up the hallway to the bathroom and hammer on the door, bellowing, "Are you done in there?" Nearly adding 'with my toothbrush,' just as Craig pulls the door open, grinning a grin so violence inducing it could be used in evidence for the accused.

"Good morning," he beams. "Bad luck last night. You really missed out. She fucks like a pro."

My mind is slow to translate, "What?"

"Oh, not Sadie. I'd give her a seven out of ten at best but, all holes. Not many girls do that. Especially on a first… date?" Craig stops to ponder this word before rephrasing, "Fuck, first fuck."

This isn't the kind of mental image I need to envisage right now. My stomach lurches again in protest. I make a mental note not to drink from the same cups as Sadie ever again.

"I really need the bathroom, Craig."

"Yeah, no problem. One question, though?" Craig leans in, his nose nearly touching mine, and breathes in my face, "Can you still smell pussy?"

"Nope," I deadpan. "Surprising, though, as I am looking at a cunt."

Craig's smile doesn't waver, neither does his proximity to my face as he raises two fingers to my nose. "What about now?" he asks, his smile nearly splitting his face in half.

The thing is, I could smell it, and this is just the catalyst my stomach needs to flick the switch from 'queasy' to full-on 'sick.' I shoulder-barge Craig out of the way, clamping an ineffectual hand across my mouth as my cheeks balloon outwards, full of hot vomit.

*

37

The Priest is laughing so hard he has to pull over.

Matt just looks disgusted.

Sam is a world away, staring out the window. He doesn't seem to have registered that the car has stopped. His eyes focus on nothing but his own reflection staring back.

The Priest wipes tears from his eyes and says, "For the love of God, you have to pre-warn me about shit like that."

The Priest unbuckles his seatbelt and gets out the car.

They sit in silence as The Priest paces up and down along the hard shoulder.

The minutes tick by.

With a final shake of his head, The Priest gets back into the car.

He points a finger at the journalist and says, "You are a danger to the very fabric of society and for that I salute you." He snaps a lazy, hand to head salute at the journalist.

"Cheers?" the journalist replies.

The Priest starts the car, indicates and fixes the journalist in the rear view. "You may continue," he laughs.

Death by Monster Truck. Pursuing the Journalistic Dream. Part Seven.

I spend as long as I can in the bathroom. Once my stomach has finished expelling its contents, I brave a shower in the hope it may wake me up and wash some of the rank aroma of alcohol infused sweat from my pasty flesh.

I know I have to get my head together. The interview is not until twelve but it's pushing ten by the time I extract myself from the shower cubicle.

I open the mirrored door of the bathroom cabinet, nearly doing a double take at the visage that greets me. I look like the kind of person normally asking if you can spare any change down the local tube station.

After a quick rummage, I locate a still sealed toothbrush and toss the one Craig has defiled into the bin. I make a mental note to do something awful to his if I ever get invited back to his flat again. Which seems unlikely after last night's fiasco in the taxi but I can always hope.

I brush, I floss, I swill mouthwash until it burns. Still, the rank taste clings to my mouth. An obscene fur coats my tongue. Its colour brings up images of disease and infection. I start to feel queasy again. I brush again, blood infused spit gracing the plughole. I floss again, depositing the long pink stained lengths into the toilet, then flush. I scrape the gunk from my tongue and find myself gawking at it, now freed from the confines of my mouth. I bring it closer to my nose. I cannot resist giving it a sniff but am left disappointed by what is largely now the aroma of toothpaste.

The taste lingers on, however. My mouth remains befouled, as if the irremovable aftertaste is my gob's way of punishing me for the things I poured into it the night previous.

Half an hour passes by the time I brave leaving the bathroom. I am barely out the door when I run into the blonde slag from Craig's flat leaving Sadie's bedroom, looking like she's been dragged through a hedge. Her appearance makes me feel a lot better about how I must look.

"Morning, Clark," she slurs, steadying herself on the doorframe and attempting, in her mind anyway, a sultry pose.

I was just going to blank her and walk past, but this comment really annoys me. Okay, in the confines of Craig's flat, and coming from the mouth of the host of the little soiree, fair enough, but coming from some dumb slag with dried seminal fluid in her hair, in my fucking flat, really pushes my buttons.

"My name is not Clark," I say, remaining remarkably calm. The blonde slag looks confused.

"But Craig called you Clark last night? I assumed that was your name?"

"Well, it's not. Clark Kent is the alter ego of superman."

"Nah, that was Christopher Reeves," she replies.

At this moment, my brain reminds me I am only wearing a towel and I really should be doing other things but the blonde slag has just touched on one of my pet hates.

"Firstly, its Reeve, not Reeves. No S."

This is a pet peeve of mine. It is Asda, not Asdas. Cliff Richard, not Cliff Richards. Stop adding fucking S's or endure my wrath.

"Whatever," she replies as she toys with a dead looking lock of blonde hair.

"And secondly," my train of thought deserts me as I stare blankly at the blonde. She stares back as equally blank as I am.

"And?" she says, thankfully breaking the silence of the stupid.

"Never mind," I sigh and wander off without a goodbye, grateful for the solitude of my bedroom.

*

Dave crosses the bridge.

It's no wonder so many people struggle with alcohol.

The keyword is struggle.

You struggle with maybe a crossword, a question at a quiz night or maybe eating a very large sandwich. Something so readily available shouldn't be a struggle.

It's easy, it's encouraged and, at the end of the day, it's another thing that'll end up getting you sacked or, worse, made to take early retirement.

Dave may be gone but his ghost lingers in The Priest's car, in his abandoned Volvo and in his old house. He leaves behind the sickly sweet aroma of stale alcohol. Spirits that a good airing and a steam clean should remove.

He was dealt an unfair hand in life and that hand was holding a drink.

Life will go on for Dave as long as his liver does, or there's always the bridge.

Later that day, while he is searching for dropped change in a nearby car park, he spots a drunken businessman failing to gain entry to his Audi.

The drunk stabs his key towards the lock and misses.

Dave watches him do this again and again, remembering his recent bafflement at the cluster of paint chips around the door handle of his own Volvo.

Mystery solved.

4.

Next stop the Clifton suspension bridge, a bridge that had already claimed two lives even before it had opened to the public. Bridges like this are part of the reason for the rise of Health and Safety in the Workplace legislation. The quickest way for the bridges painters to get to the hard to reach bits at the top was to simply walk up the giant chains that held it up. Sadly, it wasn't just workers who saw this handy short cut.

*

"I don't get why people like Dave drink. Everyone knows alcohol's a depressant," Matt says as he doodles in the condensation on the window.

"It's a social thing. If I'm at a social event, I drink," the journalist replies.

"It's the same at book launches, award ceremonies..."

"Baptisms," The Priest interjects with a smile.

Matt raises an eyebrow. "Speak for yourself Father."

"A liking for drink is one of the lesser things that could be levelled at a man in my position," The Priest says, "but we're not here to talk about the ins and outs of the priesthood, thank God."

"Is that a clue?" Matt snaps back.

"What? I'm not playing fucking Cluedo, Matthew. I'm not the kind of fellow who drops hints and poses cryptic riddles. This isn't a game here, son."

"Oh, I just thought you were hinting at what brought you here."

"The car, Matthew, the fucking car brought me here."

"But in the bigger picture there must be something that... um... you're running from," Matt replies.

"And what exactly are you running from, son? I don't see how having to deal with a handful of paperbacks stuffed through your letterbox can drive you to contemplate suicide. There are plenty of us out there who have wives that bailed, plenty of us living lives that didn't go exactly as they planned. There are even some people who can blunder on through life knowing they killed someone, never telling a soul."

41

Matt sighs. "It was a little bit more than a handful of paperbacks."

"A carrier bag's worth, then. Whatever," The Priest shrugs.

"That was to start with."

*

The man from the returns department. A short story in two parts. Part Two.

My wife always resented me. My predicament was my undoing and gifted her with the bestseller she could never write.

You know what sells? Abuse sells. Were you raped? Molested? Then write a book about it. Go into any supermarket and look at the paperback section. I can guarantee you will find at least half a dozen of these true-life harrowing tales on the shelf. It'll have a black and white photo of some dishevelled looking child on the cover, a title like *Don't Tell a Soul*, or something along those lines.

My agent showed me an early draft of her foray into misery porn a few days ago.

Did I say my agent? Scratch that. Turns out he's *our* agent now. Figures, really; made for each other, those two. Royalties over loyalties, pair of jackals the pair of them.

But I'm getting ahead of myself.

As my wife grew ever more distant, the deliveries got bigger. I got adept at the stacking of books. I had to; they were no longer coming in carrier bags in dribs and drabs but boxes full. Boxes plural, two maybe three at a time would be left on my doorstep.

After I brought them the second bag of books, my local charity shop started turning me away. I offered to sign them but they looked at me like they didn't know who I was.

Repeat this every couple of days at a different charity shop. I was stuck with them. Even worse, I noticed some of the books being delivered were the ones I had only just disposed of a few days before. Little things like inscriptions, coffee rings and bent covers.

I lined one wall of my study with them. That was actually quite fun but did look a bit like a narcissistic art installation.

I didn't notice when she left, or the kids. I think she said goodbye, I don't remember.

Ways of disposal started getting trickier. It only took the local tip a couple of visits before they barred me. Something about having to pay for commercial waste disposal, like I was a tradesman disposing of a skip full of rubble.

One night I made a bonfire but the neighbours were not happy. You live in a half a million pound house and people just don't expect the neighbours one evening to recreate *Fahrenheit 451* in their back garden.

The police arrived the following evening, fire brigade in tow. Another means of disposal crossed off my ever dwindling list for fear of prosecution.

My evenings were spent driving around looking for book banks, though I knew that they would soon be returned to me. Some nights I would drive for hours, desperate to put a bit of distance between me and the books, foolishly thinking this was a means to an end.

They would come back though, with interest.

The empty house was quite handy. I started to fill the kids' bedrooms first. Out of sight is out of mind and all that.

I stopped receiving visitors. Everyone but the man from the returns department, but he never asked to come in. He had his errands to run, drops to be make and a ledger to fill in.

The people who called were concerned, they were worried and, of course, they had spoken to my bitch of a wife. I doubt if she was concerned or worried. She was probably too busy putting the finishing touches to her book.

The house wasn't empty for long. Soon books were piled in every room. Every cupboard and flat surface used.

My options exhausted. My mind, my body exhausted. There was only one thing I could do.

*

The car pulls up at the toll barrier for the bridge.

"If you're sure Matthew, then this is where you get out," The Priest says.

"He won't stop," Matt mumbles.

The Priest nods.

*

Matt is soon a speck in The Priest's rear view mirror.

Toll paid, The Priest, the journalist and Sam cross the bridge in silence.

*

A van sounds its horn three vehicles back. The sudden noise rouses Matt from his silent contemplation beside the road.

"He won't stop," he mutters again.

The car at the front of the queue pays. The barrier rises, the car passes and the barrier falls. Everyone crawls forward.

The van honks again.

Matt strains his eyes to catch a glimpse of the idiot behind the wheel.

"No," he moans.

Matt turns and starts to run.

The barrier raises, the next car passes, the barrier falls and the line crawls forward a few feet, including the man from the returns department.

*

"So what do we all think?" The Priest asks.

"I think he's mad," the journalist replies.

"You saw the books though, didn't you?"

The journalist nods. "Doesn't prove anything. Could have gathered them up himself, given his delusion a bit of weight. I mean, he could have left them back at home, why bring them along for the ride?"

The Priest shrugs. "Maybe he ran out of room."

"Maybe it was all for show?"

"What are your thoughts on our writer friend, Sam?" The Priest says.

Sam watches the Bristol landscape streak past. "I think he was a man looking for help but instead found you."

"You say that like it's a bad thing, Sam," The Priest smiles.

Sam shrugs.

"I wouldn't be surprised if our writer friend turns up along the line with a new – what did he call it? misery porn? – creation of his own. I'm sure our journey will make a fantastic chapter before his miraculous recovery from the brink of suicide," the journalist sneers.

The Priest frowns. "Your lack of faith in Matthew disturbs me."

"Don't get me wrong, I hope he jumps. Sadly, though, like a lot of writers, he used to be a journalist and, well, journalists have a certain reputation, I should know. I don't buy it."

"Whilst we're on the subject, any chance of some closure on your wee tale?"

The journalist sighs.

Death by Monster Truck. Pursuing the Journalistic Dream. Part Eight.

My phone bleeps on the bedside table, snapping me out of my daydream of flatmate related threesomes. For this, I will be forever thankful to my battered Nokia.

I read the message, 'NATCAS ETA 12.10 S,' and then read it again until the meaning of the assorted letters and numbers resemble something that makes sense. Not the hardest text-speak to work out but, after last night's skin full, I'm just happy I can still decipher letters and numbers.

I locate my notebook, a handful of pens and my Dictaphone. It is one of the old tape versions, handed down to me from my dad. I press play to check if it still works. The wheels turn making a rather irritating squeal but fuck it. At least it still works.

I throw it into my holdall with the rest of my collective crap and spend ten minutes on my laptop reading Natalie Cassidy's Wikipedia page and ordering a taxi to pick me up. Research done, I feel ready to brave whoever may still be hanging around the flat, before I embark on my new career interviewing D-list celebrities.

I shamble into the kitchen hoping to be left alone with my hangover.

"Well, well. Who says that you can't polish a turd," Craig crows. He is alone but that's bad enough.

"Cheers. Hope I don't look too good, though. Wouldn't want you trying to fuck me as well."

"Do I detect a little jealousy?"

"Look. I don't like you, Craig, and I'm sure you don't like me. Can we cut the bollocks, cut the banter and just get on with our days. I'm sure you have a V.D. clinic you need to ring or something."

Craig holds his hands up in surrender. "Fine by me."

"Thanks," I reply sarcastically as I ram a slice of bread into the toaster a little harder than necessary.

I'm not sure if I prefer the uneasy silence to the jovial abuse slinging. For once, I actually hope Sadie will grace us with her presence.

The toaster pops and I liberally butter the toast, praying it will stay down once I have eaten it. I turn around and Craig is still sat watching me, occasionally taking a tiny sip of his drink.

"So where is she, then?" I ask.

"I really fancied a Danish pastry so she popped out to get me one."

"And the other conquest?"

"Think she went with her. Probably fighting over who gets to carry the bag."

All I can do in reply is shake my head. I am not a violent man but I really would like to punch the smug little smirk off his face.

"Can I give you a word of advice?" Craig says, leaning over the table towards me.

I roll my eyes, ready for whatever thinly veiled joke he is going to impart to me. He sees my theatrical eye rolling and frowns.

"This is in all seriousness."

"Go on," I say as I shoulder my holdall ready to leave. I grasp the strap tightly, minimising the possibilities of me swinging for him.

"It's more of an observation really. You smell like a brewery."

"Really?" I cup my free hand around my mouth and exhale.

Craig rummages in his trouser pockets and produces a packet of mints, those annoying little triangle shaped ones that come in a little dispenser, and he tosses them over to me.

I uncurl my grip from my holdalls strap so I can catch them and the bag slips down my arm and onto the hard kitchen floor, just as I remember it contains my rather antiquated dictation machine. Fuck.

I'm not sure if it's my hangover affecting my depth perception or my general ineptitude for sport based tasks, but the packet hits my out-stretched hand before rebounding on to the floor below. Craig tries to hide his amusement.

As I duck down to scoop them and my holdall off the floor, I grunt a belated, "Cheers," and make my escape.

I depress the top of the mint dispenser to no avail as I bound down the stairs. Cursing Craig's name, I give the pack a shake. It sounds like it has plenty left inside so I click again. This time it works, so I dispense a further four directly into my mouth.

The morning is grey and dull outside, much like the way my insides feel and probably look at the moment. I look both ways up the road for a taxi that isn't there and spot Sadie and the blonde slag gossiping as they stroll down the pavement, happy as two pigs in shit.

Desperate to avoid chitchat I scan the street again, praying for my knight in shining taxi to come rescue me and as if by magic one turns onto the street and starts to roll slowly down the road. The driver must be looking at the house numbers. I raise my hand in the air and wave fruitlessly in its direction. The taxi doesn't speed up any.

The inane sound of women making small talk grows ever closer from the opposite direction. I step into the road and double my efforts by waving with both arms. Still, the bloody taxi driver doesn't see me. It's going to be close. That is if this particular taxi is even for me.

"Yoo-hoo!" Sadie shouts in my direction, at last spotting me waving frantically in the middle of the street. I step back onto the pavement and flash her a smile.

"Looks like this one's mine," I say, gesturing at the approaching cab. Conversation is now unavoidable.

"I'm glad I caught you. I wanted to say good luck," she says, clumsily attempting a hug, something she has never felt inclined to do before and, to be honest, it throws me a bit.

"Um... thanks?" I reply.

Sadie pulls away from me and wrinkles her nose. "You should do something about the booze breath, though."

"I'm working on it," I say as I dispense another half dozen mints into my gob.

The blonde slag mercifully remains silent by Sadie's side, eyeing the front door eagerly, awaiting the attentions of King of the Dickheads himself, Craig.

The taxi insists on continuing its journey towards our increasingly uncomfortable conversation at a pace usually reserved for snails, slugs and poorly financed formula one teams.

"Well, this is me." I gesture to the taxi and then gesture towards the door of our flat.

Sadie rushes me for another embrace, squashing her small tits into my arm and whispering into my ear, "Don't fuck this up."

The tender moment is destroyed somewhat by the taxi driver leaning on his horn as if he has been waiting for hours. I try to shoo Sadie into the flat but she is damn well determined to wave me off like a mum watching her child take its first tentative steps at playgroup.

I climb into the taxi.

*

In Bristol you're spoilt for choice when it comes to choosing a bridge to hurl yourself off.

Their next stop is only twenty minutes away. Plenty of time for a pit stop; after all, you should never top yourself on an empty stomach. Why deny the pathologist the opportunity to work out what your last meal was?

They stop at a motorway services. A chain coffee shop, an under-staffed petrol station and a budget hotel are the highlights. This could be anywhere.

The Priest refuels the car. He pays cash.

He drives the short distance to the building that contains the usual suspects. The generic coffee outlet, the generic burger restaurant and toilet facilities that have received the piss and excrement of countless thousands of weary travellers, some of whom even managed to get it in the bowl.

Inside, a cleaner pushes a brush around the legs of tables looking for loose change. He pays no heed to the table where The Priest, the journalist and Sam sit, though he would not look out of place sat amongst them.

They order the same meal. The Priest devours his, the journalist picks at his fries and Sam stares at his blankly.

The Priest wipes a napkin across his lips and belches. "Pardon me," he says with a smile.

The journalist snaps out of his silent contemplation of his now cold fries and says, "Sorry, I was daydreaming."

"Anything good?"

"No, not really. Just going over the same old shit."

"Ah yes, the old reoccurring dream."

The journalist rubs his eyes. "The problem is when I wake up it feels like I haven't actually slept. I've been to see doctors, psychiatrists, fucking hypnotists. I've tried medications both legal and illegal, to no noticeable effect."

"And now you've sought out a priest."

"I didn't go looking for a priest though, did I?"

"No, you went looking for a solution." The Priest nods towards the bridge.

"I just want to sleep."

"Well you can't go leave us without finishing your little yarn now can you? Me and Sam have a big journey up north and I'm sure I speak for us both when I say, we're just dying to hear the rest."

The journalist laughs a mirthless laugh.

Death by Monster Truck. Pursuing the Journalistic Dream. Part Nine.

Some nights are better than others. Sometimes I have cringed myself awake by the time the redhead is hurling in my lap, sometimes it's when Craig dangles his fishy digit in my face, it's all very vomit based. When my dream slash nightmare slash total recall gets to the point I'm stepping into the taxi, I know I have to ride it out to the end. This is my penance. I have wronged and this is my punishment and I deserve it all.

As soon as I am in the taxi, I know something is up.

Sometimes you get a feeling, like a sixth sense.

I get the scent of pine cleaner trying to mask the stench of vomit.

Her Vomit.

My cum.

His taxi.

His anger.

What are the fucking odds?

It doesn't matter; they're not in my favour anyway.

"What the fuck was all that about?" asks Sadie as the taxi speeds away, moments after I have been roughly ejected onto the pavement by the burly driver for the second time in less than 12 hours.

I have no time to explain. My wristwatch insists on moving its arms closer and closer to twelve. I am well and truly fucked.

I spend the next few minutes screaming abuse at some unfortunate telephone operator. I know that this in no way will help me get another taxi but I am still in absolute denial of my own fault in the current situation.

Because of my complete absorption in berating an entirely innocent woman on the other end of the phone, I totally disregard the beeps that come from my mobile. These beeps are trying to draw my attention to my quickly depleting battery. I realise this far too late, though, as it emits its final warning of a quick succession of beeps before refusing to turn on again unless plugged into the mains.

I stare blankly at the phone before hurling it to the ground. It explodes in a shower of cheap plastic and circuitry while Sadie and pal watch my petulant little performance silently.

Not sure what to do next I neck another couple of mints before squatting down to retrieve my SIM card from what used to be my phone.

"Have you quite finished?" Sadie asks.

"What?" I snap back, letting the remains of my phone fall back onto the floor. All the king's horses and all the king's men couldn't put this numpty's phone together again.

"I said, have you quite finished?"

"I would say so. Yes."

"Good. Cos you know, stomping round like Bratzilla isn't going to get you to your interview any faster," she imparts like a teacher scalding a naughty pupil.

"Do you have any better ideas?"

The blonde slag becomes unlikely saviour by uttering the words, "I could drive you?"

I could have kissed her if the idea of Craig's cock being in her mouth didn't instantly spring to mind. I opt for a friendly squeeze of her hand.

I am in no way surprised when we arrive at a bright pink Ford Ka, false eyelashes attached to the front headlights and 'powered by fairy dust' emblazoned on the back windscreen. Inside the car is another assault of pink and faux fur, adorning the seats, seatbelts and the steering wheel. If a six-year-old girl designed a car, this would surely be the resulting automotive abomination.

"Come on!" Sadie squeals in excitement as she climbs into the back.

"Ooh! This is dead exciting isn't it," the slag adds.

"My thoughts exactly," I say climbing into possibly the campest car in existence.

"Little Mix or Adele?"

I mutter, "For fucks sake," but it gets lost in amongst the excited shrieks and opening caterwauling that masquerade as an intro for whatever girl-band bollocks is playing.

I look at my watch and pray that she doesn't own any albums by Ellie Goulding.

I am hit by the first stomach cramp just as we reach the hotel. I am late and now bent-double in agony.

Sadie chips in the obligatory, "Are you okay?"

"Fine," I gasp as the pain starts to subside. "How's my breath?"

"Probably could do with a few more mints mate," she smiles.

I fruitlessly click at the dispenser.

"Fuck. All out."

The cramps hit me again. My intestines feel like they are filled with shards of glass.

"How many of those have you had?"

"All of them," I reply.

"Oh god. You idiot."

"What? What?" I splutter as the pain increases.

"Did you not read the back of the pack?"

I read the packet.

I read about excessive consumption.

I read all about laxative effects.

I can only guess how hard it is to get dark stains out of pink upholstery, so I get out the car.

"I'm here to interview Miss Cassidy," I tell the unimpressed girl at reception. She takes in my colourless complexion, the faint air of alcohol and my generally ruffled exterior.

"Look, I'm running late."

"Yes. It is customary for the star to be the one fashionably late, not the reporter," she says without a shred of humour.

"I wouldn't really call her a star…"

"And what would we call Miss Cassidy?" someone inquires from behind me. When I say someone, though, I instantly know it is going to be her agent.

I spin round and smile weakly, attempting to think up an acceptable line of bullshit to feed her. Her arched eyebrow says it all.

"She is more of a phenomenon I'd say." I extend a hand, praying she is satisfied with my comeback.

"Miss Cassidy is waiting," she says, ignoring my outstretched hand. She turns and beckons for me to follow. She has an unusually large arse for a woman of her size.

I can feel another cramp starting to develop as I enter the suite. Her agent crosses the room and taps on an adjoining door, waits a few seconds, then opens the door and promptly disappears without a word.

I hurriedly lay out my old tape recorder and notebook just as the latest cramp doubles me over in what I imagine are child-birth strength levels of agony. I collapse onto the room's sofa clutching at my midriff, waiting for the pain to subside.

I break into a cold sweat and try to ride it out, praying the agent doesn't return to see me looking like an addict in the throes of withdrawal.

It's no good. I either make a run for the bathroom now or shit myself. Damage control wise, I choose the bathroom.

I burst into the bathroom shaking like a shitting dog and only just make it in time.

As I lower my buttocks towards the bowl and unclench, what starts off as a fart soon transforms into an unrelenting torrent of hot faeces.

The sounds and smells are repugnant. Sweat starts to drip down my face and plasters my hair to my skull as one bout is soon followed by another quick burst.

I lose track of how long I'm in the bathroom.

I forget all about the interview I am supposed to be conducting on the other side of the door.

Nothing else matters.

I start to get scared I may not be able to stop.

I start to cry.

When there is nothing left to expel, after I have opened the bathroom's small window as wide as I can and attempted to make myself look as presentable as possible, I venture back into the hotel room.

The room is empty. My notebook is discarded on the floor.

I curse my rotten luck and trudge across the room, the weight of the world weighing down my narrow shoulders. I stoop and pick up my notebook and soon realise why the room is empty.

I cannot make out if the questions are written in my hand; they are so scrawled they could be the scribbling of anyone at last night's get together.

Here's a sample, 'Was there a script in Eastenders or was it a case of who could bellow the loudest?'

And that was one of the nicer ones.

I drop the book back to the floor just as the telephone starts to ring in the corner. I bet it's for me and I bet it isn't good news.

But that's all in the past now.

People keep on telling me I should look back at it and laugh, which is a lot easier said than done when it's your own personal trauma someone is poking fun at.

I never spoke to Selena again. Never would I get to catch another glimpse of her fat tits squashed against her cheap IKEA desk. Oh well, tits are tits and they weren't the last pair I saw attempting to escape from a too tight business suit. I lived in London after all.

I would work in this town again; I'd just burnt a very large and busy bridge is all.

I found myself a fully-fledged member of The Talent Pool, with a dozen or so stories under my belt so managed to stave off Sadie's complaints about money whenever necessary.

I had to get my laptop repaired. I didn't have to look at the bill to know that I couldn't afford it.

I approached Sadie at the kitchen table and explained my situation.

She smiled a knowing smile that I was beginning to both recognise and loathe before sliding over a manila folder and tapping the white label stuck to the top right corner.

"By Tuesday alright?" she said.

I stared blankly at the title of my latest assignment.

Death by monster truck.

*

"I don't think you're going to make your deadline, friend," The Priest says, raising his cup of coffee to his lips and taking a tiny sip.

"Ha! I'm going to make a deadline alright," the journalist snorts.

"The bridge is easily reached on foot from here. Maybe the walk will do you some good."

"The fall will do me even better."

The Priest shrugs. "A change is as good as a rest I suppose."

"Change is for people who have options."

Sam gets up and shakes his head.

"What're you shaking your head at?" asks the journalist.

"You don't know you're born," Sam says.

The Priest and the journalist sit dumbfounded.

"I beg your pardon?" the journalist splutters.

Sam has already walked away.

5.

"And then there were two," The Priest laughs, aiming the car towards the slip road and accelerating hard.

Sam sits in the front seat recently vacated by the journalist.

"People say alcohol is a depressive, and rightly so; you saw the state David had got himself into. The despairs of drink are nothing in comparison, however, to a long journey confined to a lap belt." The Priest nods towards the backseat and grins. "To get someone in that central seat is the tricky part. That takes planning. It takes smarts. If the wrong person sits in that seat and doesn't get the ball rolling, you're fucked. You're just five strangers in a car looking at bridges."

"Well done you," Sam replies.

"I knew you'd be the last one, Sam. I would have put money on it if I were a gambling man. I don't do games of chance, though. I like certainties"

The car merges lanes and is back on the motorway heading north. It starts to rain.

"They'll all go to hell, Priest. You've helped them damn themselves," Sam says.

The Priest shrugs. "If they go through with it."

"Isn't that what this journey is all about?"

"Look at it like this. They're not exactly going to be an asset up there are they? A trio of miserable fucks sat on their clouds bemoaning the shit they had to endure on earth. If you think about it, I provide one hell of a service, in this world and the next."

"You call this a service?"

"I don't hear you offering to drive," he winks.

Sam shakes his head but can't suppress a smile.

"Unburden yourself, Sam."

"Ha! Where do I start?"

"I find the beginning is as good a place as any."

Big brother, the bad wife and the princess. Start.

I am from a long succession of weak men.

My father lies dying in his hospital bed, translucent skin taut across his skull and ribs. His breath is faint and pained, whistling from between pale, blood-starved lips.

My mother doesn't want to see him like this, so doesn't.

She's not weak.

I sit beside him and watch the unsteady rise and fall of his chest and wish him dead.

Occasionally he yelps, sometimes managing to form words, but mainly just stifled cries escape. It breaks up the monotony of my silent vigil.

He hangs on.

I visit daily, hoping to be greeted by an empty bed and the kind words of the nurse but instead he hangs on in there, clinging onto a life that deemed him obsolete years ago.

He opens his rheumy eyes and stares at me as if I'm a stranger.

Maybe I am a stranger today. Yesterday I was his long dead best friend; the day before that, some former work colleague.

I stare back blankly. I have no words.

A nurse comes in and reports that there has been little change in my father's condition. She mentions a hospice and her thoughts on which of my father's internal organs she reckons will betray him first.

I ask her why he screams. Can't they give him more for the pain?

She shakes her head.

Soon, I'm left alone with him again.

I take a pillow off the neighbouring bed and stand over him.

But I'm from a succession of weak men, remember?

I return the pillow to the bed and sit back down.

Visiting time ends and I return home to an empty house.

I am from a long succession of weak men.

There are always exceptions to the rule, however, and boy was my big brother an exception.

I have an idealised memory of him. The intervening years have not weathered him at all. If anything, the years have airbrushed away the errant hairs and blemishes, making him even more ethereal in my mind.

There is the truth and the reality of his story. I was too young to understand a lot of what happened and what was said at the time.

My mother would not talk about what happened so in turn my father wouldn't either.

No, what I learned was from playground taunts, half heard whispers in the classroom and from the graffiti written on cubicle doors. Not that I understood what most of it meant until much later.

My brother was murdered. His body dissected into eight pieces, placed into two suitcases and dumped in a field. He was only seventeen.

He was always arguing with our mum. Typical teenager stuff. He would come home late; mum didn't like the crowd he'd fallen in with, usual stuff. My father would cower behind her, waiting for his prompt to acknowledge that his feelings mirrored hers. Weak, weak man.

Voices would be raised, names called, accusations made, the front door would slam and my brother would disappear for a few days. He always came back though...

I would sit at the top of the stairs, rolling my cars and trucks along the patterned carpet and wait for the door to slam. In a few days my brother would come back and bring me a new car.

Some things I don't remember. He always had money but I don't remember him having a job. When he would disappear for a few days, I don't remember where he went. Maybe I didn't ask, I'd just be over the moon he'd come back. The cars helped.

He would bring home exotic American cars for me. Dinky, Matchbox and the occasional Corgi. Pontiacs, Buicks and Chevrolets would line up with the trucks and vans my parents bought me. Working vehicles for working men. Keep those aspirations in check, young man.

My brother was effortlessly cool. His look was more rocker than mod, though he didn't have the motorcycle yet. That was next on the list for him. Get his licence and buy a bike. He had the leather jacket already; no helmet of course, that would mess up his hair.

One day he didn't come home.

The usual few days turned into a week.

The days ticked by but my parents stubbornly refused to report him missing.

I'll never forget the last time I saw my brother.

Ten days after he'd slammed the back door and went wherever it was that he went, he finally turned up.

You have to remember this was the sixties. Things moved a lot slower back then.

The police were stumped. They had a body but no missing person to match it to. All the killer had left behind clothing-wise was my brother's leather jacket, and our mum had stopped writing his name in his clothes years ago, so that was a dead end.

A murder investigation was launched and the police circulated an official photo in the local press. They had taken my brother's severed head, tidied it up a bit, stuck his eyes open and put a scarf around the base of his skull before photographing it. This was the image that would grace thousands of newspapers. This would be the final image of my brother: the last place I would see his face.

He always had dreams of becoming famous and now he was, kind of.

Though the police's tactics were unusual and maybe a spot macabre, they worked. According to my parents, my father opened the paper one morning to see this awful image on page three of the local rag. I have no recollection of this.

Every following day, though, as the rumours and the gossip surrounding his murder started, I was quickly reminded of the grisly circumstances in which my brother may have met his untimely end. I grew up pretty fast after that.

I soon came to understand what *puff*, *queer* and *homo* meant. Guilt by association meant I was humiliated, beaten and taunted on a daily basis.

After all, a blameless person doesn't end up hacked into eight pieces, stuffed into a pair of suitcases and dumped in a field for some farm hand to discover, tossed under a hedge.

With my brother gone, I caved. I became a mini version of my father.

My mother was not a naturally maternal woman. But one evening, as I hid under my bed covers crying my eyes out after another torturous day at school, she did something that really surprised me.

I heard my bedroom door open and footsteps cross the room.

I froze. I dabbed the tears from my eyes with the corner of the blanket and waited for her to tear the covers away, to expose my weakness, my shame. To fix my red eyes with hers and tell me I was weak. Weak like my father, weak like my brother. Weak.

I wait.

She calls my name. Just the once and then waits.

I try will the tears to stop, the reddening of my eyes to subside and the sniffle in my nose to desist to no avail.

I slowly pull the cover from over my head and face her in all my tear-stained, snotty glory.

I stare at her defiantly.

She thrusts a hand into her apron pocket, takes out a familiar yellow and blue box and holds it out to me.

To my surprise it's a toy car; not a van or a truck, but an actual car. A pale blue Lincoln Continental with opening boot.

She tells me to take it.

I drag my pyjama sleeve across my face, smearing snot and tears across the flannelette, and swing my legs out of bed, approaching with caution.

She watches me with mild amusement as I snatch the box and clamber back into the sanctuary of my bed. She leaves without a word.

She was a funny old woman, our mother.

I sit and watch as my dying father screams at the ceiling. He has been doing this for over a minute now.

No nurses come, no one cares.

He started without warning. Just opened his eyes and started bellowing at the top of his lungs. It amazes me that such a frail body can still produce such a racket.

I sit and marvel at my father. His back arches slightly as the scream becomes a rattle. His back relaxes and with a sigh he lapses into sleep or maybe unconsciousness once again.

The nurse comes in and asks me to sign some forms, which I do without reading them.

She talks at me, telling me nothing new, then leaves.

Screams start from another room up the corridor, this time a woman.

My father stirs and sees me, though if it is me in the traditional sense is up for debate, and he mumbles an apology.

I ask him what he is apologising for and he starts to cry again.

I ask him again, more angrily this time.

"Everything," he says.

The headmaster looks scared and he should be.

My mother rarely comes to the school. I have brought myself back and forth since the age of eight. Parents' evenings are attended by my father alone.

My mother tells me to undress.

Shamefaced, I peel off my grey jumper, unbutton my shirt and fold it carefully over the chair beside my mother.

She holds a hand up, indicating for me to stop.

My arms are bare and covered in bruises, both elbows have abrasions.

She asks him what he is going to do about this.

The headmaster talks about rough and tumble, boys being boys and that there are always two sides to every story.

My mother unfolds a newspaper cutting and carefully places it in front of him.

She taps the newsprint with a finger and asks what the other side to this story is. Even though it is upside down, the picture of my brother's dressed head is unmistakable.

It didn't matter how many times you saw it, it never failed to shock. The headmaster fumbles his glasses off his face, fiddles with his buttons and hastily rearranges some nearby paperwork.

My mother asks what is to be done but doesn't like the reply.

She tells me to take off my trousers. I do so, revealing bruises and welts that run from the top of my legs to my ankles. I stand there and shiver, awaiting instructions.

She tells the headmaster that this must stop.

He agrees but gives no indication to how this may be achieved.

Later that day my mother sorted it out once and for all.

As soon as I saw my mother in the playground after school, I knew something was going to happen.

She wasn't there waiting for me. She looked through me and searched the faces of the other boys in my class. One boy slowed his pace and let the other kids pass him, quickly falling behind.

The terrified child started to scan the playground for his own parents. He spotted his mother in amongst a gaggle of nattering housewives oblivious to his presence.

My mother started to move towards the boy. He turned and looked back towards the door he had left by. The headmaster stood there, eyes fixed on the ground. By the time he had turned back round my mother was upon him.

The boy looked up at my mother's furious face and wordlessly confirmed his guilt.

She nodded and pinched his ear between her finger and thumb. As he wriggled and writhed, she dragged him over to the no longer nattering housewives.

The boy's mother started shrieking for her to unhand her child, which she did once she was in front of the woman.

Calmly, she asked if she was the boy's mother

Amongst an expletive laden reply, the woman confirmed that said child was indeed hers.

My mother then broke the woman's nose with a single punch.

59

No one tried to stop her; no one jumped in or threw a punch back. It was over before it had begun. My mother was already striding out the school gates as two friends helped the stunned woman to her feet.

When I got home I waited and waited for a knock at the door, expecting to witness my mother being taken away in handcuffs. The police never came and more importantly, no one ever laid a finger on me at school again.

That night my mother came into my room and sat on the end of the bed. Without looking at me she said that there would come a day when I would have to fight my own battles and clean up my own messes.

I often wonder if that day ever came.

*

The miles tick by as the light begins to fade. Cities and towns become clusters of lights in the distance. Cars pass by like shadows, revealing nothing about the lives contained within their metal bodies. Trucks rattle past in bursts of noise and spray.

The steady thump of the windscreen wipers, back and forth, accompanies the roar of the engine as the only soundtrack within as Sam falls silent.

The Priest pushes the cars cigarette lighter in, then searches for his smokes, patting at his clothes with his free hand.

"You know there was nothing you could have done regarding what happened to your brother, right?" he says as he fumbles a crumpled pack of cigs from a shirt pocket.

Sam shakes his head. "It's not about my brother."

"Just out of interest, was anyone ever charged with his murder?"

"No one was even arrested, let alone charged."

The lighter pops out of the dashboard as The Priest places a cigarette between his lips.

Sam blankly stares at the dashboard.

"Could you be an angel and get that for me please, Sam?"

Sam pulls the lighter from the dashboard, flipping it round to look at the business end. Watching the glowing orange rings cool and fade to black.

"If it's the whole situation with your dying father, most of us probably would have considered, ahem, helping him on his way," The Priest says, holding his unlit cigarette out to him.

Sam plucks it from his hand, sticks it in his mouth and lights it. He inhales deeply, collapsing into his seat, eyes closed.

"They never bring their own fags," The Priest mutters.

Sam exhales.

"You forget. I'm from a long succession of weak men."

The Priest shrugs and holds his hand out for his cigarette. "You're not exactly lap belt material though, are you now?"

Sam takes another long draw on the cigarette.

"Ah come on now, Sam," The Priest replies, "don't make me beat it from you."

Sam snorts. "What? The story or the cigarette?"

"I'd be lying if I said it wasn't close," The Priest says, holding his hand out impatiently.

Big brother, the bad wife and the princess. Middle.

My father steadfastly refuses to die.

My employer is no longer as understanding. "Take as long as you need" – their words not mine – has now changed to "When can we expect you back?"

The simple answer is, when he dies. Give or take a few days to bury him, mum can sort the rest. I've done my bit tenfold.

He never calls for her, never mistakes the nurse or my daughter for her, and doesn't ask me why she isn't there.

Instead he asks for the football results, which I make up whilst pretending to read from the paper.

He nods as I tell him that Wolverhampton Wanderers destroyed Nottingham Forest in a six goal romp. He asks who scored and I make up a name at random. He tells me to keep an eye out for him. One day he'll be playing up front for England. You mark his words.

His eyes glaze over and he looks past me, my cue to leave.

I stand up and take my coat off the back of the chair.

He continues to stare at the wall; his bottom lip starts to tremble.

I wave a hand in front of his unblinking face, put my coat on and leave.

I pass a room where an old lady sits staring at her hands. Turning them over, back and forth, marvelling at her wrinkled flesh. Her expression is one of mild bafflement and joy.

As I reach the double doors at the end of the ward my father starts screaming again.

I return home to find the usual mix of bills and junk mail on the floor. I scoop them up and carry them to the kitchen, tossing them onto the breakfast bar.

I flick the kettle on as I check the answer phone.

Today's missed calls consist of someone from H.R. asking me to call back regarding my return to work, a handful of pitches from cold callers and the dreaded weekly message from mother. Though when I say message, it is more a list of errands, repairs and unspecified tasks she expects me to do for her on my next visit.

The kettle boils; tea is made and left to cool as I leaf through the pile of mail.

The letter addressed to my wife stops me mid-leaf. I read her name again and place the letter on the counter, separate from the others designated for the bin.

I wander aimlessly around the house until I find myself in front of the mirrored wardrobe in our bedroom.

I slide the door across, revealing dresses, blouses and formal wear not worn for years. Boxes of shoes line the bottom, the lids heavy with dust.

Before I know it I'm looking out the window at the ruins of what was our back garden.

The police had dug it up five or six years ago looking for her, finding nothing.

I always assumed one day she would come back.

At least one of us knew she wasn't buried in the backyard, but the police, eh? They never take your word for it though, do they? You're innocent until proven guilty, though I hear they can prosecute without a corpse nowadays. The worst they found was a long-dead family pet called Mr Flopsy. Natural causes, if you must ask.

The only crime scene left behind was the one they made of my back garden. I never put it right, didn't see why I should. Though I doubt the police have a dedicated branch for landscaping and horticulture.

Maybe first we should hear my side of the story, eh? If only to pass the time, because people don't just disappear do they?

I let the first woman I ever loved slip away.

Youthfulness and stupidity seem to go hand in hand, don't they? We drink until we fall down, take unnecessary risks with our own personal safety and, when offered unconditional love, we do our best to sabotage it.

My friends had a hand in it. They would mock me, bang on about first sowing my wild oats. Oat sowing is highly overrated in my opinion, as are friends.

She was the one and I drove her away. That much I know.

This letter is not for her though.

The passage of time has robbed me of everything but fleeting dreams where I see my idealised version of her face, her body, her.

Her birthday is lost to me. I no longer recall her middle name, things that once seemed so important, all gone. She is now reduced to a few bullet points and this flawless, ageless dream that always smiles, always laughs and forgives me without question.

This letter is not for her.

I wouldn't even know where to begin to start looking for her.

Besides, look at me now. A weak, old man pining after a woman he threw away decades ago.

No, I don't know where she is because I was an idiot.

No one has ever dug up my garden looking for her, though. Lucky escape, eh?

I met my wife at work.

She was the pretty receptionist, probably far too young to be dating an old drone like me. I was the shy older guy, punching above his weight.

We were never meant to be but sometimes, if you're determined, stupid or maybe a little bit of both, you can make it work... for a while anyway.

I don't know why she married me. Scratch that, she married me because I loved her. I loved her without question and with blind devotion.

We learn from our mistakes and I would be damned if I let this one get away.

This time I would follow my heart.

This time I wouldn't listen to my friends. Ignore them all.

This time it would be different.

Oh, it was different alright.

We can skip the arguments about money, about her numerous infidelities and the arguments for argument's sake.

We can fast-forward a decade and survey the damage.

I find myself in front of the mirrored wardrobe in our bedroom.

I slide the door across, revealing dresses, blouses and formal wear. Boxes of shoes line the bottom. On the top shelf there is a gap where a suitcase once was.

It's all I need to see to know that she's gone.

Our daughter, all of five years of age, enters the room and takes my hand in hers. She looks up at me and asks me why I'm crying.

I tell her it's because I am a weak man.

She nods and asks for a glass of milk.

I dread facing mother.

She kept out of it. Let me make my own mistakes.

She heard all the whispers, the rumours and even saw my wife's cheating ways first hand. In a small town like this, with a network of gossipmongers that can gather and share information better than the KGB, FBI and MI6 combined, nothing is secret for long.

Approaching mother's house, I know she'll be waiting behind the front door or she'll already be stood in the doorway, arms folded. She won't ask for details, she'll already know.

Maybe she'll know more than I do. She'll never say.

She'll be there to listen and nod, all the while secretly knowing that she could have told me so, that she knew it would end like this. She won't need words; she can say it all with just one look.

They were different times.

Women would sometimes run off with their fancy man. Husbands would keep the ones that stayed in check with the back of their hands, and what would be classed as abuse today was simply called disciplining your child.

The police wouldn't come round and dig up your garden either, without good reason, and they had good reason not to dig up ours, believe me.

You see, it seems my darling wife was a little too friendly with the local constabulary. No one wants an investigation when the last notch on the bed post happens to be top brass.

It was a can of worms nobody wanted to open for fear of what else might crawl out.

It took fifteen years, a bit of gossip and a backhoe to change all that.

Like I said, they found nothing.

After all, I am a weak, weak man.

*

"I'm going to have to ask, Sam," The Priest says, "did you kill your wife?"

"No," Sam replies.

"Now you wouldn't go lie to a priest now would you?"

Sam smiles, "Scout's honour."

The Priest frowns. "People have affairs, Sam, lots of them. A failed marriage doesn't make you a failure; it just means you made a mistake. Not worth topping yourself over."

"It's not about that."

"Well it better not be about the bloody garden, Sam," The Priest laughs.

"Do we have long?" he asks.

The Priest shakes his head.

Big brother, the bad wife and the princess. End.

My father babbles at me. His eyes mad with panic. He has no idea where he is or who I am.

I have been told that he has only hours to live but mother still won't come.

This night will be his last. I have been told so by the nurse.

Mother won't come as she is busy sorting out another mess on my behalf.

I'm so tired.

I had a letter from work this morning telling me how they look forward to my return to work on the date they have decided for me. They look forward to seeing me at my return to work interview. I can bring a union representative if I wish.

They're all heart.

I'm too tired to be angry.

My father has tired himself out and lies there, wheezing.

I slip into sleep, hypnotised by the steady rise and fall of his chest.

There are two people, both in shadow. One stands at the bottom of a flight of stairs, the other at the top. Between them, at the top of the stairs, are three suitcases of descending size.

The person at the bottom looks upwards as the figure at the top steps forward, raises their knee and places their foot on top of the large suitcase.

Voices and light from an unseen room make the person at the bottom look round. As soon as they do this, the person at the top starts rocking the case with their foot, back and forth, until the case overbalances and falls down the stairs.

The case jerks down the steps. A weight shifts uneasily within and stops it from gathering momentum.

It reaches the bottom but remains upright. Blood seeps from the zip and begins to pool. The case's contents bulge and strain against the zip.

At the top of the stairs, the figure retreats back into the shadows.

Two suitcases remain.

The voices stop and the house plunges back into silence and shadow.

Finally, the zip breaks and its contents spill forth.

The figure at the bottom of the stairs stands in a pool of blood and toy cars.

I wake to screams.

Not just my father's. The whole hospital seems to be in unison, a shared pain, from the cries of distant, hungry infants to the diseased and incurable begging for death.

Outside darkness has crept into the corners. The sun hangs low in the sky. The shadows stretch and darken; merging into one another as the sun surrenders and the dark swallows all.

My dream has already started to fracture and fade.

What's left of my father is reduced to sniffs and whimpers.

I decide to take a trip to the coffee machine. I can already feel my eyelids becoming heavy.

As I walk up the corridor I see a little girl sat on a chair. Her legs swing back and forth with gay abandon. They don't touch the floor.

She watches me approach and waves.

She says 'Hello,' like we're old friends.

I stop. Her eyes are massive, drinking me in.

I say 'Hello' back to her.

She tells me that she's not allowed to talk to strangers.

I tell her that a man of my age isn't supposed to talk to little girls.

She giggles and swings her legs back and forth.

She asks why?

I sit down next to her and tell her I don't know why. Maybe it is because there are bad people out there.

She asks me if I'm a bad person.

I tell her that I don't think I am.

She nods.

I ask her where her mum and dad are.

She laughs and asks me where mine are.

I tell her my dad is in the room up the corridor, dying.

She asks me why.

I tell her she asks a lot of questions.

She tells me I have a lot of belly.

We both laugh.

I tell her that she reminds me of my daughter.

We are alone in the corridor. The mixed smells of antiseptic, bleach and disinfectant make my head spin. I start to wonder if I'm dreaming again.

She asks about my daughter and I tell her that she was my princess. She tells me this is awesome, that princesses are awesome and, therefore, I must also be awesome.

I sigh and tell her that though being a princess sounds kind of awesome, eventually you grow out of it.

The little girl frowns.

I tell her that sometimes princesses don't want to be princesses anymore. Sometimes they grow up.

She asks at what age do people stop wanting to be princesses. I can see tears in the corners of her eyes. I am now the man who dismantled the castle, drained the moat and sold the talking candlestick.

I tell her that my daughter will always be a princess to me.

She asks me what she is now.

I stop and mull it over. I tell the little girl that my daughter is a model.

She asks if she models clothes.

Sometimes, I reply. Sometimes.

I make my excuses and leave.

My daughter may have been born out of some misguided desire to save an un-saveable marriage, but she was always loved.

That kid may not have saved my marriage but she saved me.

When her mum left, I don't know what I would have done if it wasn't for her. This is why she will always be my princess.

She needed me, she loved me and we were each other's world. Sounds corny, I know, but it's the truth.

67

I did the best I could and when I needed some help there was always mother. There are some things that even the most doting of dads cannot help with.

You hear horror stories about teenagers but that's all they were to me, stories. She never once stayed out late, didn't ring when she said she would, or throw a house party. You couldn't have asked for a better child.

You can't have this kind of luck without it going to shit somewhere though, can you?

I lay the blame firmly at the door of her ex-boyfriend.

He knew she was too good for him so went about treating her like shit, making her think she didn't deserve any better. An unusual tactic but you'd be amazed-slash-horrified to see just how many times this works.

He was, is, and probably always will be a work-shy piece of shit. Thinks he's an artist after spraying – sorry, tagging – the side of some building. When he's not doing that, you can find him mooching around the town centre chatting up school girls and buying them cigarettes.

My princess saw this quasi-gangster, clad in the finest leisurewear the dole can buy, walking down the street with a half-limp, half-just–shit-myself lollop and thought, yup, that's my kind of guy.

You can tell I wasn't a fan.

During their brief dalliance he took some pictures.

The plastic cup burns my hand. How the plastic doesn't melt is a mystery.

Coffee in hand, I am heading back to my father's room.

The little girl is still sat on the too big chair, swinging her legs back and forth. She waves as I approach.

I wave back with my free hand.

She tells me she has a present for me. She holds something tightly in her fist.

I ask her what it is and she uncurls her tiny fingers to reveal a toy car. A pale blue Lincoln Continental with opening boot.

I tell her that I had one just like it when I was a child.

She nods.

I ask her where she got it from.

She shrugs and says she doesn't know. She asks where I got mine from.

68

I take the car from her open hand and run it across my leg. It's uncanny; the car looks like it just came out the box, though it must be over forty years old.

I tell her my mummy gave it to me.

She nods.

I ask her if she's sure I can have it and again she nods.

She pushes off the chair and lands with a bump. She smoothes out the creases in her clothes and gives me a smile.

I thank her for the car.

She shrugs and skips off down the hallway.

I run a finger over the paintwork of the car and the paint flakes; old, tarnished metal shows beneath.

I look up but she's already gone.

There are two people; one in shadow, the other is me. I stand at the bottom of a flight of stairs, the other person at the top. Between us, at the top of the stairs, are two suitcases, one larger than the other.

I look upwards as the figure at the top steps forward, raises their knee and places their foot on top of the larger of the two suitcases.

Voices and light from an unseen room make me look round. As soon as I do this, the person at the top starts rocking the case with their foot, back and forth until the case overbalances and falls down the stairs.

The case jerks down the steps. A weight shifts uneasily within and stops it from gathering momentum.

It reaches the bottom but remains upright. Blood seeps from the zip and begins to pool. Like before, the case's contents bulge and strain against the zip.

One suitcase remains.

The voices stop and the house plunges back into silence and shadow.

Finally, the zip breaks and its contents spill forth.

I stand at the bottom of the stairs as blood pools round my feet and look up.

The person at the top steps forward again and I see her face.

The screams wake me again.

My coffee is now cold.

Outside is darkness pricked occasionally by the orange glow of a street light.

My father's screams are laboured, with a distinct rasp and a rattle now.

I think about my princess. How I wanted so much better for her. She's as bull-headed as her mother was; like her grandmother, too. Thank God she wasn't a boy.

Mother will sort this out, she always does.

Oh, they'll probably shout and bawl at each other, doors will be slammed and names called, but I wouldn't be surprised if right now they're sat sharing a pot of tea, dabbing away tears and making good. Mother always finds a way of you seeing it from her point of view.

I bet she wouldn't be taking the kind of shit I'm getting from work with a smile, no chance.

While I've been daydreaming about mother putting the sword to the H.R. department, I haven't noticed that my father has stopped screaming.

He raises a shaky hand and points towards the old toy car that I have put on the table beside his bed. Tears roll down his face.

I pick the car up and hold it out to him.

His bony fingers curl round the toy car and he shakily withdraws his arm.

Raised voices from an unseen room make me look away.

The voices abruptly stop and my father suddenly starts to convulse and gasp.

I get to my feet and approach the bed. His mouth is agape.

I shout for a nurse and pull the emergency cord by his bed.

He bucks and gurgles, thrashes and retches, all the while with his mouth wide open.

I step closer, catching a glimpse of something in his mouth. The back end of a pale blue Lincoln Continental with opening boot protrudes from the back of his throat.

When the nurses enter they find me with one hand rammed into my dying father's mouth, the other pounding on his chest.

There are two people; one is me, the other is my mother. I stand at the bottom of a flight of stairs, my mother at the top. Between us, at the top of the stairs, is a small suitcase.

I look upwards as she steps forward, raises her knee and places her foot on top of the suitcase.

Voices and light from an unseen room make me look round. As soon as I do this, my mother starts rocking the case with her foot, back and forth until the case overbalances and falls down the stairs.

The case jerks down the steps. A weight shifts uneasily within and stops it from gathering momentum.

It reaches the bottom but remains upright. Blood seeps from the zip and begins to pool. Like before, the case's contents bulge and strain against the zip.

The voices stop and the house plunges back into silence and shadow.

Finally, the zip breaks and its contents spill forth.

I stand at the bottom of the stairs as blood pools round my feet and look up.

She turns her back and walks away.

I wake to my own screams.

The waiting room the nurses took me to is dark and silent.

A seam of light marks the outline of the door as I get up and stumble blindly across the room.

The bright light of the corridor dazzles me as I emerge.

At one end of the corridor a policeman talks to a nurse. They see me and begin to whisper.

I start towards my father's room. The policeman falls into step behind me. His pace quickens as I approach the door.

The room is empty.

The policeman has some questions.

They always do.

I re-read the instructions for the payphone a second time. I feel sick, I'm tired, and my father is finally dead.

Mother has to be told.

I manage five numbers before I slam the receiver back into the cradle. How do I deliver this? What do I say? Where do I start? Do I mention the car?

The policeman watches me from across the room, once again whispering to the nurse.

I'm sweating. I can feel each bead of sweat being tracked by his watchful gaze as they roll down my face.

He swaggers across the room towards me.

I put the receiver down and pretend to search my pockets for something.

He asks me if everything is alright.

I laugh and say that I've forgotten my mother's phone number.

He watches me intently and nods.

I say that I should know my own mother's phone number.

He agrees. I should know my own mother's phone number.

I laugh nervously and shrug, adding that it's probably down to the shock of what's just happened.

He nods again and takes out his notebook. He leafs through the pages, then stops. He taps his finger against the page before holding the notebook towards me.

There are three numbers printed: my own, mother's and my daughter's.

I ask why he has my daughter's number and he shrugs. He says he is exploring all avenues, being thorough, just doing his job.

I thank him and start to type in mother's number again.

The policeman doesn't leave, however. He frowns and reads his notes again.

I hang up the phone before it has time to ring and ask him, if he doesn't mind, I would like a bit of privacy.

The policeman looks up from his notes and apologises.

He has only taken a few steps away when he stops and turns.

I ask him what he wants now.

He says it's probably nothing but when was the last time I spoke to my daughter.

I shrug and tell him this morning.

He asks if she is the kind of person to not answer her phone, maybe if she didn't recognise the number.

I shake my head and say no.

He shrugs and says maybe she's dead.

I take a step towards him and ask him to repeat what he just said.

He looks confused and says maybe her phone's dead.

Approaching mother's house, I know that she'll be waiting behind the front door or she'll already be stood in the doorway, arms folded. She won't ask for details, she'll already know.

I feel sick.

I have driven through red lights, sped over zebra crossings and failed to give way to get here, though I fear time is against me.

I run up the path and hammer on the front door, nearly shaking it from its frame.

Mother answers the door and hisses at me to get inside.

I step inside and look around. I spot the pink suitcase straight away.

Mother just stands there, arms crossed, her face expressionless. I fall to my knees and start to cry.

She tells me to get up.

She tells me to shut up.

She tells me to listen.

She talks about honour.

She talks about family and shame.

She talks about death.

Turns out the police dug up the wrong garden.

Turns out my brother did come home.

Now it's my turn to put things right.

The suitcase is empty. Mother nods towards the living room.

I stumble across the hallway and open the door. My daughter lies motionless on the sofa. She looks so peaceful.

Mother nods and goes to the kitchen.

*

You cannot fail to be impressed by the Humber Bridge. It dominates the skyline, demanding your attention regardless of what angle you approach it from.

It's a very popular destination.

The Ford Granada pulls over.

"Time's up," The Priest frowns.

Sam gets out the car and walks away.

The Priest jumps out after him. Light rain speckles his glasses.

"Are you just going to leave it at that?" he shouts after Sam.

Sam keeps walking. Soon he is lost to the darkness.

"Sam," The Priest shouts.

He ducks into the car and flashes the high-beams down the road, catching a faint glimpse of Sam in the distance. He honks the horn in a series of short blasts.

"Damn it," The Priest spits, wiping his glasses on his shirt.

He revs the engine unnecessarily and pulls out without indicating. He crawls along the inside lane flashing the high-beams, looking for Sam, but to no avail.

Sam has gone.

*

He drives like a demon. He commits to no one lane. He continues north blind with anger, crossing the border at speed. The night streaks into the dawn streaks into the blinding sunshine of morning.

He tears off his collar and throws it in the back seat.

He shouts and curses, pounds the steering wheel with his fist.

He has no time to react when the man jumps from the overpass above and into his life.

73

The sunroof explodes in a shower of blood and glass.

Arterial blood splatters every surface; the jumper's free arm whips around the interior manically. The Priest is shoved to one side, pegged in between the man and the driver's side door. He tries to regain control of the car as blows rain down on him from the flailing arm.

The car lurches into the crash barrier, a tire explodes on impact. Plastic trim shatters in a shower of silver and black, spraying the carriageway like a bust piñata.

The car bounces off the barrier and goes into a spin. It careers off the road and rolls sideways into a ditch. The car comes to a rest in a cloud of steam, the man's protruding legs weakly kicking the crisp morning air.

People start to pull over, getting out of their cars and watching from a safe distance.

The crumpled front end oozes fluids while one remaining windscreen wiper, bent and broken, waves back and forth at the gathering crowd. The legs sticking out the sunroof stop moving after one final jerk.

The crowd grows but no one dares come any closer.

Sirens soon approach.

The Priest sleeps for a long time.

He doesn't dream within his medically induced coma.

He should be dead.

He awakes broken but alive.

He can feel the screws, the metal plates and each developing scar.

He can't feel his legs.

A dry, rasping laugh escapes him.

He journeys back south.

He is wheeled from hospital to ambulance and from ambulance to institution.

Back to where the electoral registry says is home.

Physically, he won't get any better than this.

Mentally, he is still the mental health services' problem.

He is sectioned, drugged and monitored.

The days roll onwards with little happening to help differentiate between them.

At a quarter past eleven The Priest rolls himself out of the unit to smoke a cigarette. He does this every day like clockwork.

There is a bench that he parks himself next to. Beside the bench is a bin with an ashtray on top, the black plastic body scarified by a hundred carelessly stubbed out cigs.

He reaches into his pocket and takes out his tobacco tin and lighter. From within the tin he takes out his pills from the previous day and drops them into the bin. He selects one of the many roll-ups he has pre-rolled whilst the rest of the hospital was asleep, pops it into his mouth and lights it.

"Tastes like freedom," The Priest laughs.

He is joined by various patients, orderlies and the occasional delivery driver. Each hurriedly smokes their cigarettes without making eye contact or conversation, then leave.

"What happened to your legs?"

The Priest looks up.

A young woman points her cigarette at his legs.

"I beg your pardon?"

The girl rolls her eyes. "Your legs, what happened to them?"

"They don't work," The Priest replies.

"Well, duh. Why don't they work?"

The Priest shakes his head. "You're a very straight-to-the-point kind of gal, aren't you now?"

"I find it better to be direct in a place like this." She takes another drag on her cigarette. "You going to tell me then, or do I have to beat it from you?"

The Priest smiles. "You wouldn't beat a man in a wheelchair now, would you?"

"Fuck it. If the story was interesting enough I'd use the chair to beat it from you."

"I'm guessing you're a patient?"

The woman laughs. "Hopefully not for long. This place is full of lunatics."

"What's your name?" he asks.

She smiles. "Honor, and if you laugh I *will* beat you with that chair."

"Tis a beautiful name."

"Cheers," she laughs and playfully punches him on the shoulder. "Who are you, then?"

"They call me The Priest."

She snorts. "Well, I'm not calling you that."

He shrugs.

She mirrors his shrug and says, "I shall call you Wheels. Yes, Wheels until you furnish me with your real name."

"I've been called worse."

"I bet you have. Come on then. Introductions are done and dusted, get with the story."

The Priest checks his watch. "It'll be lunch soon, maybe later?"

She rolls her eyes. "Well, we wouldn't want to miss that now, would we?"

"Okay. You'll get a kick out of this no doubt. I got in a car crash. I'm driving along and, bang, someone smashes through the sunroof, just jumped off an overpass, couldn't of timed it any better. I lose control of the car, pinball it across the carriageway and end up on my side in a ditch. Woke up in the hospital full of metal and minus the use of my legs"

She thinks for a moment. "That is both hilarious and terrible."

"Yup, someone up there has a plan for me. One that doesn't include me using my legs, it seems."

"Come on, let's go have lunch. I'll push," she says.

He stubs out his cigarette and flicks it into the bushes.

"So you going to tell me what brings you to this fine establishment?" he asks.

"I doubt you'll accept ambulance as my answer, right?" she says, wheeling him back into the hospital. "If I was to pigeonhole it, I suppose I'd have to go with: I had a little bit of a breakdown."

"Well, I'll understand if you don't want to talk about it."

"Nah, In fact, you may get a kick out of my little tale," she laughs. "Do you like horror?"

The Priest shrugs. "I like a good story."

"Well mine has it all."

They roll into the cafeteria and load up their trays. They find an empty table in the corner.

"Should I risk eating first?" The Priests asks with a smile.

"I think you'll be able to keep it down but I make no promises."

"That's what the lunch lady said," he laughs.

"So I wake up on a sofa, no idea where I am. The room swims and spins. I throw up and crawl towards the door...

*

The hallway is familiar, though rarely viewed from this angle.

I know I've been drugged and I start to cry.

My hand slips out from under me and I fall on my side. My hand is wet. I bring it to my face. The palm is covered in blood.

My eyes focus. I lie in a pool of it. I push myself up onto my knees and vomit again.

Drag marks in the blood streak towards a door at the end of the corridor.

I follow the blood. No idea why, all I see is the door.

I push the door open. I know this room. I know this kitchen. I try to stand, pulling myself up. The blood is everywhere.

I head towards the light of the back door.

It takes forever to cross the room. Broken crockery and glass crunch beneath my feet.

I fling the door open and the light hits me like a punch to the face.

I fall. I vomit. I cry. I sleep.

I wake in the afternoon. My head is clearer now, though the feeling I have is worse than any hangover I've ever experienced.

I know where I am though. I know this garden.

I'm at Grandma's.

I can stand but every step feels like someone is punching me in the base of my neck.

I slowly make my way back towards the house.

The kitchen is a bloodbath. I pick up the phone and take it outside. I sit on the back step and call the police.

I babble away into the phone. The poor woman on the other ends tries to make sense of me and tries to calm me down but I'm going a million miles an hour. I mean, who could blame me? I'd woken up in a fucking abattoir.

It's the police who point out the suitcase to me. My pink suitcase, abandoned at the bottom of the garden. We approach it in a group.

Someone has written on it with a black marker pen in big capital letters: 'DIG HERE.'

I don't see them dig up the remains but the police tell me to prepare for the worst. They'll have to run some tests but they believe the bones to be that of my missing mum.

They take me to hospital and pump my stomach as a precaution. While I'm there they tell me that my Dad is missing and wanted for questioning. They find Grandma in the boot of Dad's car a few days later, chopped into eight pieces and stuffed into a pair of suitcases.

I think it was when they told me about Granddad that I finally snapped.

*

The Priest finishes his soup and wipes round the bowl with a piece of bread.

Honor leans in and whispers, "Wanna see something gross?"

The Priest shrugs and says, "Go on, then."

She digs in her pocket and takes out an old toy car. A pale blue Lincoln Continental with opening boot.

He looks at the car blankly.

"You know where I got this from?" she smiles.

He does but he shakes his head.

"The police gave it to me. It was my dad's. Do you know where they found it?"

He does but again he shakes his head.

"They found it rammed down my Granddad's throat."

"Well they do put warnings on these things nowadays," he laughs.

She stares at him angrily.

"Sorry. That was in poor taste."

She nods and places the car on the table.

"I'll do the jokes, Wheels," she replies, forcing a smile.

"It's a pretty weird thing to carry around," The Priest says.

"It reminds me of dad. They never found him. I just wish I could see him again. Ask him why he did what he did; to say goodbye."

"Maybe he wasn't the type of chap for goodbyes."

She shrugs. "Maybe. I was his princess, though."

The Priest nods and asks, "Tell me, my dear, can you drive?"

*

Honor turns out to be the ideal student.

Though there will be less room in the next car, The Priest's work will continue.

They scour the message boards, the chat rooms and social media, and pick their trio carefully.

A new car is sourced, this one without a sunroof.

The date is set and they head to Beachy Head together.

*

"They're late," The Priest fumes.

"Well, you're the one who put all those rules and regulations on how they could get here," Honor replies. She perches on the bonnet and stretches.

"That's how I've always done it. There's no need to deviate from a tried and tested plan."

"Why here?" she asks.

He shrugs. "Why not."

"I'm going for a walk, you want to come?"

He checks his watch. "Go on then. It's been a while since I last stretched my legs."

She slides off the bonnet and helps push his chair.

"I'm always surprised how people in wheelchairs manage to keep their hands looking clean," she giggles as they bump over the grass.

"Not too near the edge please, Honor."

"Don't worry, you're in safe hands."

They stop by the edge and listen to the waves crash on the rocks below. She takes the old toy car from her coat pocket and hurls it into the sea.

The Priest nods.

She stares out to sea, pulls her coat together to keep out the cold, and says, "It's no wonder people kill themselves here."

The Priest laughs. "There's nowhere to go but down."

"What do you reckon happens?" she asks.

"When you die?"

"Yeah. Do you think there is more than this?"

The Priest shrugs. "It'll be a nice surprise if there is."

"You said it, Priest," she replies.

She grabs the wheelchair and pushes The Priest over the edge, chair and all.

He falls for twelve seconds. He doesn't flail or scream.

She turns and waves to a man watching her from the car park and shouts, "Was that okay, Daddy?"

Other novels, novellas and short story collections available from
Stairwell Books

Carol's Christmas	N.E. David
Feria	N.E. David
A Day at the Races	N.E. David
Running With Butterflies	John Walford
Poison Pen	P J Quinn
Wine Dark, Sea Blue	A.L. Michael
Skydive	Andrew Brown
Close Disharmony	P J Quinn
When the Crow Cries	Maxine Ridge
The Geology of Desire	Clint Wastling
Homelands	Shaunna Harper
Border 7	Pauline Kirk
Tales from a Prairie Journal	Rita Jerram
Here in the Cull Valley	John Wheatcroft
How to be a Man	Alan Smith
A Multitude of Things	David Clegg
Know Thyself	Lance Clarke
Thinking of You Always	Lewis Hill
Rapeseed	Alwyn Marriage
A Shadow in My Life	Rita Jerram
Tyrants Rex	Clint Wastling
Abernathy	Claire Patel-Campbell
The Go-to Guy	Neal Hardin
The Martyrdoms at Clifford's Tower 1190 and 1537	John Rayne-Davis
Something I Need to Tell You	William Thirsk-Gaskill

For further information please contact rose@stairwellbooks.com

www.stairwellbooks.co.uk
@stairwellbooks